KU-614-497

Tina's
Dangerous
Secret

· HILDA STAHL ·

Tina's Dangerous Secret

Tyndale House
Publishers, Inc.
Wheaton, Illinois

Second printing, June 1981

Library of Congress Catalog Card Number 80-53247
ISBN 0-8423-7211-3, paper
Copyright © 1981 by Hilda Stahl
All rights reserved.
Printed in the United States of America.

Dedicated with love to
John and Judy Raabe

• CONTENTS •

ONE

Forbidden Date

"Where do you think you're going, Tina Lambert?"

Tina whirled around and glared at the tall boy. "Mind your own business, Phil Rhyner!" She doubled her small fists and stood with her booted feet apart, trying to ignore the hard lump in her throat.

"I heard Steve tell you to stay home while he went to town."

Tina lifted her rounded chin. "I know what Dad said. I'll do as I please!" She would not think about Dad going to see Mary Lockwood again today. Tina wanted to keep her mind completely on riding to Tanner Hill to meet Dallas Tromley. "Go back to work, Phil. You don't want to waste Dad's money, do you?" She saw the red flush spread from his neck up over his face. Muscles tightened in her back and neck. She had to get away from the ranch before she burst into wild tears and completely embarrassed herself.

"It's too bad Steve didn't take you over his knee when you were younger. I sure feel like doing it right now!" He stepped toward her and she jumped back in alarm.

"Don't you touch me! Go back to training Dad's horses!" Why was she taking her hurt out on Phil? He was her friend! Abruptly she turned away. "I'm taking Blaze for a run. I'll be back later."

"Tina." His voice was as soft and gentle as when he talked to a nervous filly. "Tina, I want to help you. Let me, please."

She closed her eyes tightly against the tears that threatened. She would not turn around and let him see how upset she was. He would try to persuade her to obey Dad. "I'm going for a long ride," she said sharply. "I don't need your help. I don't want your help!"

"Don't do anything foolish, Tina. Just remember that your dad has every right to fall in love with Mary Lockwood. He's been lonely long enough."

Tina wanted to scream at Phil and beat her fists against his thin chest that he'd been working so hard to build up, but she didn't want him to see how close to crying she was. Why couldn't he just leave her alone? What gave him the right to talk to her about her own private affairs?

She jerked the reins loose from the top rail of the fence and leaped into the saddle. Leaning forward, she urged Blaze into a run. Wind whipped her long brown hair back. The June sun burned against her already tanned face and arms.

At last she felt free. She pulled Blaze to a walk and managed a smile. It would be wonderful to ride with Dallas Tromley. She knew she looked pretty in her jeans and blue plaid shirt. He would never find out that she was not sixteen as she'd told him last week, but thirteen. She shrugged. She looked sixteen, so she might as well say she was.

What would Dad do to her when he found out she'd disobeyed him? At times he could be very strict, especially since he'd fallen for all that church stuff.

"You're too young to date, Tina," Dad had said two days ago. "Wait just two more years, honey. Don't grow up too fast."

"But I don't want to wait, Daddy!"

"I know you're physically mature, but that doesn't mean you're emotionally mature. You need a couple of more years under your belt."

"I'm thirteen, Dad! Not twelve any more. Do you know how many girls in my school have been dating since they were eleven?" She had looked up at him with her big blue eyes and squeezed his hand.

"Those girls aren't my responsibility. You are. I will not allow you to go out with a boy. No! And none of that begging and teasing will change my mind."

She had turned away in frustrated anger,

knowing that this time he really did mean no. On other matters, she'd often been able to change his mind.

"I don't care what he says! If he goes with Mary Lockwood even when he knows I don't want him to, then I can go with Dallas Tromley or any boy I want to go with!"

Blaze tossed his black head up and down and almost jerked the reins from Tina's hands.

"I'm just talking to myself, Blaze. Don't get riled." She flipped her long brown hair over her slender shoulders. She would have fun today! She shielded her eyes and looked for Dallas. Would he really come? Maybe he had learned that she'd lied to him about her age! Her heart seemed to stop at the thought. "He won't find out." She shook her head.

Tina dismounted at the barbed wire fence where the Lambert property touched Codge Farenholz's ranch. Blaze lowered his head and chomped the tall grass.

A dog barked in the distance and Tina knew it was Jim Bridger, Codge's dog. It would be terrible if Codge saw her meet Dallas Tromley. Codge would tell Dad for sure. Nervously Tina rubbed her hands down her jeans. What was keeping Dallas?

Was Dad sitting in the Old Home Cafe right now having coffee with Mary Lockwood? Maybe even holding her hand? Tina frowned. Why hadn't Mary stayed out of their lives? She had convinced Dad to go to church with her. It was all her fault that Dad was mixed up with those religious people. Now all Dad could talk about was Mary Lockwood and Jesus.

Tina stamped her small booted foot. Dad might make her go to church with him, but he sure couldn't make her like it!

At the sound of hoofbeats Tina looked up expectantly. She took a deep breath and forced herself to appear calm. She was afraid her heart was beating so rapidly that Dallas might think she had a frog in her pocket. She'd given up carrying frogs around almost a year ago.

Tina licked her suddenly dry lips as Dallas pulled his bay mare to a stop. He leaped off and Tina thought she'd faint on the spot. How handsome he looked in his blue jeans and yellow and blue plaid shirt! "Hi," she said breathlessly.

"Hi." He grinned down at her and she felt very small and feminine. He had to be at least six feet tall. "Been waiting long?"

She shook her head. What warm brown eyes he had! She wanted to touch his dark brown hair. Would he want to kiss her? Abruptly she turned away with a pretense of patting Blaze. It would be so embarrassing if he tried to kiss her. She didn't know how and she didn't want him to find out.

"Do you still want to ride to Tanner Hill and do a little exploring, Tina?" His voice was a soft slow drawl and she wanted him to keep talking. *He* wouldn't tell her she should stay home until her dad said she could leave.

Tina pushed the thought of Phil Rhyner away. "If you don't want to go, we won't, Dallas." She knew she sounded breathless and she wanted to bite her tongue off. Why couldn't she sound calm?

"Sure. I want to. I haven't had a chance to see much of the countryside since we moved here. I've been mighty busy helping Ma get the place in shape."

Tina lifted Blaze's reins. She thought about the tired gray-haired woman she'd met in church last Sunday, and couldn't picture her having Dallas as her son. Tina had heard that Mr. Tromley had walked out on them about seven years ago. They didn't know if he was alive or dead. Oh, poor Dallas! At least she knew her mother was dead. She hadn't just walked out on them. She'd drowned in a flash flood four years ago while visiting her sister.

"You're very quiet, Tina," said Dallas, resting his hand lightly on her slender shoulder. "Is anything wrong?"

She liked to have him touch her but as she turned to him he dropped his hand. "I was thinking that we're a lot alike. I have Dad and you have only your mother."

"Yeah. It's hard. I look at kids who have both parents and I watch them and think how it would be if I did. Dad left so long ago I hardly remember him." She saw the sadness in his eyes and wished she hadn't said anything.

"I'm used to it being just Dad and me. I don't want it different."

Dallas lifted his eyebrows. "I saw him with Mary Lockwood a couple of times. You sure he won't marry her and bring her home as your new ma?"

"No!" She stood with her fists doubled, her eyes flashing bluer. "He wouldn't dare!" She flushed at his startled look. "Sorry, Dallas. Can we talk about something else?"

He grinned. "For such a little girl you sure do have a temper."

Her eyes widened. Who had told him? "What do you mean 'little girl'?" she snapped.

He held up his hands and backed away. "Don't turn your guns loose on me, Tina Lambert. I just meant you're little. You don't even reach the top gripper on my shirt." He laughed and she forced herself to join him. Playfully he ruffled her hair. "Shall we ride to Tanner Hill?"

Tina swung into the saddle and watched as Dallas mounted. He could ride as well as she. Dad had said she'd learned to ride before she could walk.

Suddenly Tina threw back her head and laughed. She was free! She was with Dallas! Dad would not find out that she'd disobeyed him. Phil wouldn't tell on her. He hadn't yet in the year he lived with his Uncle Slim on the Lambert ranch.

"What's funny?" asked Dallas with a frown.

"I'm happy, Dallas! Can't you just feel the happiness in the air?"

He reached out and caught her hand in his. "Now I feel happiness."

She looked down at her small brown hand in his, then up into his face. Her heart skipped a beat and her stomach tightened. "I'm glad I'm with you today, Dallas."

"I'm surprised Steve Lambert would let his little girl go out with a poor guy like me."

Tina flushed and pulled her hand away. "Don't talk like that, Dallas. I like you."

He smiled and she liked him even more. "We're going to have a lot of fun today, Tina. I know we are."

Tina laughed breathlessly. She felt as if she'd just stepped on a cloud.

TWO

The Evil Plan

"Did they really mine gold here?" asked Dallas as he stood beside Tina at Tanner Hill.

"Yes. About a hundred years ago. See that mine entrance?" She pointed to a dilapidated, boarded-up mine entrance built into a hill. "Once men found gold in there. It's really spooky walking inside." A ground squirrel raced in front of the mine opening and into the tall grass. Tina flinched, then laughed. "I get kind of jumpy around here."

"I'd like some of that gold." Dallas walked close to the entrance and touched the rough, weathered lumber. He traced the D on DANGER KEEP OUT. "Is there any chance of gold still being in there?"

Tina shook her head. "Lots of people tried in the past. Codge Farenholz talks a lot about this mine. His grandpa was killed working in there."

Dallas turned to Tina, his eyes dark with excitement. "Do you know Codge Farenholz?"

"Of course. Everybody does. He's lived on that old place of his all his life and he's seventy-some." She looked up at him questioningly. "Why?"

He shrugged. "Just interested in everybody who lives around here." He caught her hand. "Let's explore."

Blaze nickered from under a tall cottonwood where he grazed beside Dallas's bay.

"I think Molly likes Blaze," said Dallas as he walked around the hill, swinging Tina's hand back and forth in his.

Tina stopped and knelt in the sand. "I found a silver dollar right about in this spot a few years ago. I still have it. I wonder what we could turn up with a metal detector. I'm sure lots of people have thought of the same thing." Tina sifted sand over her hand. She looked up to find Dallas looking at her with a strange expression on his face. "What's wrong?" She stood up and he stepped close until he was almost touching her. Her heart leaped and she could barely breathe.

"How does it feel to have all the money you'll ever need?"

She blinked. She hadn't expected that! "I don't know. I never think about money."

"You'd have to if you didn't have it. I'd give anything to have enough money to do anything I wanted to do." His voice was harsh and she felt a cold chill slide down her back.

"Money isn't everything, Dallas. Look! We're having a wonderful time right now and it didn't cost us a dime."

He laughed roughly. "Can we walk inside the mine?"

"Not without a light. I didn't bring a flashlight or a lantern. We could come again and walk inside." And she wanted to be with him again—no matter what Dad said! But did he want to be with her again? Maybe he didn't like her as much as she liked him.

"Let's go sit in the shade and talk." Dallas caught her hand and they walked to one of the large cottonwood trees.

Tina looked up, remembering the times she'd climbed them, enjoying every minute of it. Dad had teased her about being his little squirrel. He had said he wouldn't worry about it, though, until she started storing nuts away.

Tina frowned. Why had she thought about that again? She didn't want to think about Dad today. He sure wasn't thinking about her. He was probably still with Mary Lockwood.

"You're quiet again, Tina. Is something bothering you?"

Should she tell him? It would be wonderful to share her feelings with someone. "I feel sad once in a while." She couldn't tell Dallas her troubles. Maybe when they knew each other better.

He gently brushed her hair back from her face and she was too startled to move. She looked into his eyes and breathlessly suggested they sit down under the tree.

"In a minute, Tina," he whispered. He touched his lips to hers and she closed her eyes, hardly daring to breath.

So, this was kissing!

"You're pretty, Tina," he said softly.

"So are you." Oh, dear! Why had she said that? She wanted to take those dumb words back but it was too late. Couldn't she at least have said he was handsome? She started to say something but he kissed her again. All thoughts left her head. She liked the warm feeling spreading through her. When he stepped back she looked at him with stars in her eyes. Could he tell that she loved him? Did he love her or did he just like kissing?

She sat beside him with her back pressed against the rough bark of the tree. What should they talk about, now that they'd kissed? Was there an after-kissing conversation? Oh, what would he do if he learned that she was thirteen instead of sixteen? Would he care?

Dallas took her hand and absently rubbed the back of it. "Someday, Tina, I'm going to be rich. I'll be able to take you in an expensive car to an expensive restaurant in the city."

She knew she'd be happy going to Old Home Cafe in Braden. "I like it just like this," she said softly. A meadowlark warbled nearby and Tina felt as if it was a special concert just for them.

"I hate being poor!" Dallas tightened his hold on her hand. "I hate living in the country in that run-down ranch house."

Tina tried to think of something to say but she couldn't, so she laid her other hand on his clenched fist. It seemed to relax him a little.

"But I won't have to be poor for long!" He grinned and his eyes sparkled. He turned to Tina. "I'll have money enough to get away from here until I can find a good job in Denver. Or maybe I'll go to California." He laughed. "With money, I won't have to settle down until I want to."

"But, Dallas, I want you to stay here." Tears pricked her eyes. She couldn't lose him now!

"With money I can do whatever I want, even if it means staying here!"

"How are you going to make money? Do you have a summer job at one of the ranches around here?"

He smiled at her eagerly. "It's money that I won't have to work for, Tina. It's a great plan!"

"What?" she asked with a hesitant smile. He looked excited, but something was making her feel a little uneasy.

A plane flew overhead, then all was quiet.

"If I tell you, will you promise not to tell?"

She nodded, her hands locked together in her lap. She curled her toes inside her boots.

Why was she afraid to hear his plan?

"Two guys from town and I are going to help ourselves to some money that's just asking to be taken."

"What guys? What money?" she asked sharply. Nervously she pushed her long hair out of her face.

"You wouldn't know these guys. Larry Postma and Carl Spence."

Tina gasped. "Don't get mixed up with them, Dallas. They've been in and out of jail for years."

He frowned. "Don't be down on them because of that. I like them and they're willing to let me in on their plan."

"It has to be a shady deal for them to bother with it." Tina pulled her knees up under her chin and cradled her legs with her arms. She could not stand to think of Dallas having Carl and Larry as friends.

"I didn't think you'd understand," said Dallas angrily as he turned away. "You don't know what it's like not having any money, and knowing you're never going to have it unless a deal of a lifetime comes along."

His anger hurt her and she moved closer, laying her head against his back. "I'm sorry, Dallas. Don't be mad at me. I want to hear your plan. I won't get upset again. I promise." She felt the muscles in his back relax and she moved away and waited until he turned around. "Please—tell me."

He touched her hot cheek, then smiled. "We're going to dig up a treasure that's hidden in a man's yard."

Tina stiffened. "Whose yard?" Her head seemed to be spinning. She was afraid of whom he'd say.

"You wouldn't want to know that, Tina." He jumped to his feet and pulled her up with him. "Let's ride back. I don't want your dad mad at me for keeping you away from home too long. He might not let you come again."

Tina caught Dallas's hand. "Whose yard, Dallas?" A cold knot tightened in her stomach.

"I won't tell you, Tina. Stop asking!" He frowned and tried to pull free.

"Is it Codge Farenholz?" He couldn't mean Codge! Her legs felt weak as she saw the look on his face. He didn't have to say. She knew he meant Codge Farenholz. "Don't do it, Dallas," she whispered hoarsely. "He's a harmless old man who doesn't want to keep his money in a bank. Don't try to take it! Please, don't!"

Dallas jerked away and stood with his hands on his narrow hips. "He's an old man, Tina. He doesn't need that money. I do! Carl and Larry do! We won't hurt the old guy. We just want his money."

"He won't let you take it! Don't you think others have tried? Dallas, he shot a man right in his yard about six years ago. His dog Jim Bridger is trained to attack on command!"

Gently Dallas cupped her face in his hands.

"Don't worry about me, Tina. I can take care of myself."

She caught his wrists. "Please, please don't do it!"

"Why?"

"I don't want you to. I love you!" Oh, why had she said that?

His face softened. "You do?"

"Yes," she whispered. Tears blurred her vision. "Promise me you won't rob Codge."

"I can't!"

She closed her eyes, then opened them, blinking away the tears. "At least promise me you'll talk to me when you're ready to do it. I want another chance to try to change your mind. Promise!"

He took a deep breath. "I promise. It won't do you any good, though."

Slowly she walked toward Blaze. Even with Dallas beside her the happiness had gone from the day.

Dallas caught her arm and swung her around to face him. "Don't forget you promised not to tell."

"I know," she said tiredly.

"Cheer up, Tina," he said softly. He pulled her close and pressed his lips to hers.

She pulled free and caught up her black gelding's reins.

THREE

Unwelcome Guests

Tina watched Dad anxiously as she waited for him to ask her where she'd been—and then was angry because he didn't. Before Mary, he'd been interested in everything she did. It would serve him right if she announced that she'd ridden with Dallas, that he'd kissed her! Maybe then he could get his mind off Mary Lockwood.

"Where's Mrs. Evans?" Tina asked suddenly as she looked around the kitchen. At this time of day Mrs. Evans was always in the kitchen fixing supper.

Steve Lambert set his glass of ice water on the table and leaned back in his chair. His blue eyes were serious as he looked at Tina. "I found a note from her when I got home a few minutes ago. Her daughter decided to have her baby early. Mrs. Evans had to go to Cheyenne to take care of her. She'll be gone at least three weeks."

Abruptly Tina sat on the oak chair across

from Steve. "Does that mean I'm to do the housework and cooking now?"

"You said you'd do it, Tina. It's too late to back out. I know you can handle it. We don't eat much and we don't make too much of a mess in the house."

Tina wrinkled her small nose. "I know I can do it, Dad. I just didn't expect to until next month."

The phone rang and Tina jumped nervously. Dallas wouldn't call her, would he? She tried to grab the phone but Steve reached it first. Was he expecting a call from Mary Lockwood?

Tina hurried from the kitchen, her hand pressed to her throat. She would not listen to Dad talking to Mary! Tina touched the piano that Mom had played so beautifully. Mom would not want Dad to love Mary Lockwood. Oh, how could he?

With her eyes closed Tina remembered sitting on the piano bench beside Mom while she played and sang. The song echoed around and around inside Tina's head. The love and laughter that Tina remembered on Mom's face brought hot tears to her eyes. Why had everything changed?

Tina walked to the front room window and looked across the wide green lawn to the winding driveway. She had finally gotten used to having just Dad. Now, Mary Lockwood had to butt in.

Strong hands gripped Tina's arms and she gave a little shriek and jerked away. She turned, then laughed nervously. "Don't do that, Dad."

"You're as jumpy as that palomino filly. What's bothering you, little girl?"

She frowned. "Don't call me little girl!"

Steve pushed his long fingers through his dark hair. "I don't know what to make of you anymore, Tina. I can't do anything right in your eyes."

She turned away and stared at the stone fireplace at the end of the large room. It wouldn't do any good to ask him to turn back the clock to when she'd been happy. He would give her the same old answer; real happiness is in knowing Jesus. Just someone else to mess things up.

"Would you like to know who called?" Steve walked behind his favorite blue chair.

She was afraid to ask, but reluctantly she did.

Steve rested his hands on his narrow hips. "We're going to have company tonight."

Tina locked her fingers together and looked at the floor. Oh, please, not Mary Lockwood!

"Your uncle Harold had to go to New York on business, so Edith is bringing the kids and is planning on staying until the business trip is over."

"Oh, no!" Tina slapped her hands to her cheeks. "I can't stand to have Rita and Rob here for such a long time. Dad, you know how they act! You didn't say they could come, did you?"

Steve frowned. "Easy does it, Tina. Of course I said they could come. I haven't seen my sister in a year. I want them to come."

Tina bit her lower lip to keep from saying more. Dad could not be tackled when he was in this mood. How could she live with Rita treating her like a baby and Rob acting like a baby?

"Now that Rita is fourteen and Rob twelve, you might enjoy having them around. Family is important, Tina. And we don't have a big one like some of the people we know."

With a deep sigh Tina finally agreed that she'd try to get along with Rita and Rob. She really did like Aunt Edith, so it would be nice to have her around.

By nine o'clock Tina had the spare bedrooms ready and a light snack fixed. She made a face as she thought how terrible it would be to have to share her bedroom with Rita. How could she stand it?

"They're here, Tina," called Steve from the front porch.

Reluctantly Tina walked outdoors. Phil waved to her as he walked toward the small house he shared with his uncle. Tina lifted her hand half-heartedly. She had avoided Phil since she got back from her ride with Dallas.

He might be able to guess too much just by looking at her.

"It's good to see you, Edith," said Steve, hugging her tightly. "You look as pretty as ever."

"Thank you." She stepped back from him, her head tilted. "You look very satisfied with yourself, Steve. I'm glad to see the loneliness gone from your eyes."

Tina wanted to run back into the house, but she forced herself to greet her aunt with a hug.

Edith held Tina back and stared at her. "You've grown up, Tina. I can't believe that skinny little girl in braids is you." Edith turned to Rita and Rob beside her. "Look at Tina, children. Isn't she beautiful?"

Tina wanted to sink through the ground. She lifted her rounded chin and stared right back at Rita and Rob.

"She looks the same to me," said Rita sharply.

"She does not!" cried Rob, his eyes wide.

Tina laughed. Rita had grown, too. Rob's hair looked brighter red and curlier than ever. Freckles completely covered his face and arms. He was almost as tall as Tina. Rita seemed to think being a half a head taller was something to be proud about. Her long auburn hair curled prettily around her slender shoulders. Too bad she wasn't covered with freckles!

With a warning look from Steve, Tina politely showed her guests to their rooms. Reluctantly she led Rita to her room.

"Do I have to share your room?" asked Rita in horror.

"Sleep in the barn if you want," snapped Tina.

Rita pushed her peach blouse into her white pants. "I didn't want to come. Mom made me! I'm still so mad I could walk home!"

Tina's anger left. She understood how Rita was feeling. Tina sat on the edge of her bed. "I guess we'll just have to try to make the time go faster."

Rita studied her closely. "Do you have a boyfriend?"

Tina remembered Dallas's kiss, and smiled. "Yes."

Rita stepped closer. "I do too. Mom doesn't know about him. Oh, I hated to leave. I just know that terrible Mia Jenkins will take him away as soon as she finds out I'm gone for a while."

"You can always take him back when you get home."

Rita frowned thoughtfully. "You're right, Tina." She sat beside Tina. "Can you introduce me to some boys while I'm here?"

Tina tried to think of all the ugly boys she knew. Finally she smiled. Phil wasn't ugly, but she'd introduce Rita to him. That would keep Phil from trying to run her life. "Dad has a boy working for him that you haven't met before."

"Is he cute?"

Tina frowned thoughtfully. She hadn't thought about that before. "Yes, I guess he's cute. He's fifteen, tall, blond curly hair, hazel eyes. And he works out to build up his muscles." Tina almost laughed at the excited expression on Rita's face.

Too bad she couldn't find some man who would be interested in Mary Lockwood. Most of her problems would be solved if Mary fell for another man. That would only leave Dallas and his terrible plan to take care of.

Abruptly Tina pushed herself up. "I fixed something to eat for you if you want it, Rita." This was not the time to think about Dallas's plan. Tonight she had to pretend to enjoy her guests.

FOUR

Mean Tricks

Wearily Tina walked into the dining room carrying a tray of glasses filled with ice water. She set them on the table then shook her head impatiently. "Who turned Dad's coffee cup upside down?" She picked it up, then leaped back with a loud scream as a large, hairy spider sprang out at her. The cup landed on the carpet but didn't break. Tina pressed her hand to her heart and stared at the spider on the floor near her sandaled foot.

"What's wrong?" asked Rob innocently from across the room—too innocently as far as Tina was concerned.

She glared at him. "You did that, didn't you, Rob? Pick up your stupid spider and stop playing tricks on me." This was the second trick he'd pulled on her so far. The first one had been a rubber snake in her boot. She had chased him outside into the yard and around the house until she'd caught him. She'd beat on him until he'd laughingly said he was sorry and wouldn't do it again.

"That isn't my spider," said Rob, spreading his hands out and lifting his red eyebrows. "It must be Mom's." He doubled over with laughter. "It *is* Mom's."

"What is mine, Rob?" asked Edith as she walked in, carrying a large bowl of mashed potatoes.

"That," said Tina coldly.

"Robert Mitchell Larsen! Get that THING out of here right this minute!" Edith stood back, eyeing it apprehensively.

Rob sighed. "It isn't real, Mom. You don't have to be afraid of it." He picked it up, then thrust it into Tina's face. "See, it's not real."

She screamed and hit his hand. "You'll be sorry, Rob! Wait and see." She would get him somehow and it would be a good one.

"Where's Rita?" asked Edith, looking around. Her light brown hair was mussed from working. A smudge of flour made a white blob on her forehead. She brushed her hands down her flowered apron that covered bright pink slacks and a light pink tee shirt.

"Rita's outdoors with Phil," said Rob, rolling his eyes. "She took one look at him this morning and fell in love!"

"Oh, Rob!" Edith shook her head. "Call her in for dinner, please. And if you see Uncle Steve, tell him too."

"He's in his study," said Tina, looking at the

closed door of the study. He'd said he was going to give Mary a quick call. Couldn't he get through one day without talking to or seeing her?

Several minutes later Tina thankfully sat down to dinner.

"Before we eat, let's ask the Lord's blessing on the food," said Steve, smiling from one to another around the table.

Tina saw the surprised looks on her cousins' and aunt's faces. Quickly, she bowed her head before they looked at her.

As Steve prayed, Tina felt the same odd feeling inside that she always felt when he prayed. It seemed strange to hear him talk to God as if they were friends.

"When did you start all this?" asked Edith as she helped herself to buttered peas.

"A few months ago," said Steve.

Tina wanted to crawl under the table as he told about learning that God loved him, about accepting Jesus as his personal Savior. She wanted to scream at him to stop when he said he'd never been happier. *She* was not happy!

"Do you go to church too?" asked Rita, looking strangely at Tina.

"Yes," mumbled Tina. Why didn't they drop the subject?

"If it makes you happy, Steve, I'm all for it." Edith smiled as she blinked back tears. "Lately I've been watching a man on TV who talks about a God who still works miracles, and who loves us individually. To tell you the truth, I've been interested in hearing more."

"That's good. Tomorrow is Sunday, and we'll all be going to church." Steve reached for the platter of fried chicken. "You and I will have a long talk later, Edith."

Tina was thankful when they started discussing the horses that Steve raised, trained, and sold. That was a conversation that Tina could enjoy.

"This Mary Lockwood you mentioned, Steve." Edith looked at Steve and Tina hated to see the flush on his face. "Is she married?"

"No." Steve picked up his glass of water and drank it quickly.

Tina wanted to yell at him for acting like a little boy in love. She knotted her fists in her lap. "She's an old maid. She's at least thirty-five years old!"

"Tina!" Steve frowned at her. "Mary's a wonderful woman. She's kind and generous as well as beautiful."

"Aha!" Edith nodded and smiled. "Do I hear an interest in her?"

Tina wanted to shout no, but she didn't dare. Dad just might send her to her room, and that would be humiliating in front of Rob and Rita.

"I met Mary at school. She teaches kindergarten. During summer vacation, she's the town librarian. I want you to meet her, Edith. I think you'll like her."

Tina forced down her food, wishing she were on Blaze, riding across the pasture with the wind whipping her hair back and blowing away all her heartache.

Later Tina stood beside the corral with Rita and Rob. It was good to be outdoors!

"I want to ride Blaze today," said Rob firmly. "Why do we have to wait until you feel like it, Tina?"

Tina rubbed the white mark on Blaze's face. She might as well let Rob ride. Maybe then he'd leave her alone.

"Someone's driving up the driveway," said Rita, turning to watch.

Tina's heart missed a beat as she watched the old flatbed truck with the faded red cab bump and rattle to a stop beside the machine shed. Codge Farenholz climbed out with Jim Bridger beside him. Abruptly Tina turned away. She didn't want to think about Codge or his dog.

"That man looks like an old-time rancher you see on TV westerns," said Rob in a low voice. He chuckled. "And his dog is sure a funny mixture of colors."

"Do you want to ride or not?" snapped Tina, glaring at Rob. "You can't keep your mind on one thing for even a second!"

"What'd I do now?" Rob scratched his red curls.

After putting the bridle on Blaze, Tina

swung the saddle into place. "Here, Rob. Grab that strap and tighten it up."

Rob reached under Blaze's stomach and tried to grab the cinch strap. Every time he reached under, Blaze stepped forward, almost knocking Rob down. Tina giggled. She'd get Rob yet!

"Hold Blaze still, Rita," snapped Rob impatiently.

Rita nervously clutched Blaze's bridle, standing in front of Blaze. Tina knew that at a command from her, Blaze would stand absolutely still. She stood beside the wooden fence and watched.

A fly landed near Blaze's eye. He shook his head and Rita screamed, dropping the reins.

Tina held the bridle and waited until Rob had the strap cinched. She couldn't wait until he mounted. Hiding a grin, she helped Rob onto the black gelding's back, then handed him the reins.

"I don't know what to do," said Rob anxiously.

"Just hang on." Tina slapped Blaze on the rump. "Get up, Blaze." She chuckled as Blaze trotted around and around the corral. Dust filled the air and she sneezed.

"Hang on tight, Rob," shouted Rita from her perch on the top rail of the fence.

Suddenly the saddle slipped and Rob cried out in fear.

"Don't just stand there, Tina," shouted Rita angrily. "Help Rob before he gets hurt."

"Whoa, Blaze," commanded Tina, forcing back a laugh as the saddle slipped to the horse's side and Rob still clung tightly. "Whoa, boy."

With a groan Rob dropped to the ground. He leaped up, his face as red as his hair. "You did that on purpose, Tina! I know you did!"

Tina slid the saddle back in place and tightened the cinch. She finally turned to Rob. "I said I'd get you."

He sputtered, then burst out laughing. "You sure did, Tina. You got me real good. Now, can I learn to ride?"

Tina stared at him in surprise. She had thought he'd never want to climb on a horse again. She suddenly smiled at him, a real smile from her heart. "Sure, Rob. You won't have any trouble this time. Just sit in the saddle and get the feel of Blaze under you. Later you can ride in the open." She could not believe what she was saying. Was she beginning to like Rob?

She stood beside the fence and watched as Rob rode around and around. She jumped when Rita slid down beside her.

"I think you're mean for pulling such a terrible trick on Rob. I'm going to tell your dad!"

"Don't be such a baby, Rita. He asked for it."

"And Tina Lambert's just the one to give it to him."

Tina turned and stared at Codge Farenholz. She saw the laugh lines around his eyes. His battered old Stetson was pushed back on his bald head. "You could do it even better, Codge." It was hard to tease with him when she knew Dallas and his friends were planning to rob him—maybe even hurt him.

Codge chuckled. "I reckon I could at that, little girl."

Reluctantly Tina introduced Rita and Rob to Codge. She knew they thought he was a weird old man who dressed funny.

Codge tongued his chew of tobacco into his other cheek. "You kids don't want to let this little wildcat get the best of you. Just send her to me if she does. Me and Tina understand each other." He winked, then tugged his hat low over his eyes. "Tell Steve I bought a fancy saddle over to the auction the other night. He might be interested in buying it."

"I'll tell him, Codge." Tina could barely talk around the lump in her throat. Why didn't she run after Codge and warn him before he climbed back in his truck? But she thought of Dallas and how much she loved him and she knew she couldn't break her promise to him.

"What's wrong, Tina?" asked Rita sharply. "You look sick."

Tina glared at her, her hands on her slender hips. "Leave me alone, Rita! I am not sick!" Tina saw Phil walking toward them and she called him over.

"Phil, teach these guys to ride, will you? I've got better things to do."

"Like learning how to be polite?" asked Phil as she walked past him.

She glared at him, then ran to the house, dust puffing onto her boots from the driveway.

FIVE

Mary Lockwood

Tina leaned weakly against the handrail as she fought against the tears that had been trying to fall, first in Sunday school and then church. It was getting harder and harder to shut out what Megan Clements, her Sunday school teacher, and Pastor White said about Jesus. Tina didn't want to think about Jesus. It just made things seem more mixed up.

Slowly Tina walked to the bottom of the steps. Next week she'd be sick so she could stay home.

"Tina. Tina!" Rita hurried down the church steps, her soft green dress swishing around her legs. "Was Dallas here today? I want to meet him."

Tina frowned. "Not so loud!" She should not have told Rita about Dallas, but somehow she'd started talking in bed last night. It had been easy to share secrets in the dark of her bedroom, and it had felt wonderful to tell someone. She shouldn't have trusted Rita!

"Is he here?" whispered Rita, looking at the crowd of people coming from the church into the bright sunlight.

Tina rubbed her hands down her denim skirt. "He's here, Rita. But just shut up about it, will you? You're going to make trouble for me."

"Oh, but I want to meet him!" Rita's blue eyes sparkled.

Tina's heart leaped as Dallas walked up to her and said hello in a voice that sent shivers up and down her spine. "Dallas, this is my cousin Rita Larsen." Tina said a whole lot more but she couldn't hear her own words in her excitement. Dallas was close enough that she could reach out and touch his tan shirt or rest her hand in his.

When Phil joined them she forced herself to stand quietly and talk in a normal voice. She did not want Phil to learn that she liked Dallas. Phil just might tell Dad.

Tina was glad when Phil finally walked away to join his uncle. He made her feel very uncomfortable.

"I wish Ma would hurry," grumbled Dallas, frowning as he looked up at the church. "She always has twenty people to talk to. I'm starved."

"Here she comes now," said Tina breathlessly. "I'll see you, Dallas."

He smiled down at her. "I'll see you, Tina."

Tina watched until he slid into the driver's seat of a dusty blue car. She wanted to wave and throw him a kiss but she didn't dare.

Rita grabbed Tina's arm. "Is that Mary Lockwood standing beside Uncle Steve?"

Tina nodded, then turned quickly away.

"Oh, she is beautiful! I like that pink dress she's wearing. I wonder how I would look in short curly hair." Rita moved closer to Tina. "I can tell she likes Uncle Steve by the way she looks at him."

Abruptly Tina walked toward the parking lot. She would not listen to another word about Mary Lockwood.

The heat inside the car made Tina gasp. She held the door open and waited a few minutes before sliding in. She was glad Rita had not followed her.

She leaned her head against the back of the seat and closed her eyes. It felt strange to sit in the back. Soon Rita and Rob would push in beside her and Aunt Edith would sit up front with Dad.

Children's shouting and laughter filled the air. How would it feel to be a little girl again?

The front car door opened and Tina jerked up, her eyes wide. Oh, no! Mary Lockwood stood beside the car with Dad!

"Mary's coming to dinner today, Tina."

"I hope you don't mind." Mary's voice was soft and musical. She slid in the front seat and Tina knew it wouldn't matter if she minded or not. "Your dad told me you're doing a wonderful job around the house since Mrs. Evans left."

Tina mumbled an answer as Rob and Rita noisily pushed into the back seat. As soon as Edith closed her door, Steve started the car and slowly drove from the parking lot. The air conditioning soon cooled the car enough to make it comfortable.

The conversation between Edith, Mary, and Steve drummed against Tina's ears, and she wanted to cover her head. Rob tried to talk to her but she snapped at him.

"Tina," said Steve in his warning voice.

Tina slumped in her seat and wished she had the nerve to make him mad. If Mary saw what a temper Dad had, she might lose interest in him.

She was out of the car and into her room before anyone could speak to her. By the time Rita walked in, Tina was dressed in her blue jeans and light blue tee shirt. It would be terrible to work in the kitchen with Mary always trying to help, probably pretending it was her kitchen.

"Is Dallas coming over today?" asked Rita as she pulled jeans from her dresser drawer.

"How should I know?"

"Don't snap my head off!"

Tina rushed from her room and ran straight into Steve.

"What's wrong, honey?" He held her lightly,

looking down into her face. "Why the tears?"

She brushed them away. "I'm . . . I'm so miserable, Daddy! Nothing is right anymore."

He pressed her against his shoulder and she smelled his after-shave lotion. "I know everything is different, little girl. But we must keep on living. I'm happy, Tina. I want you to be."

"I can't be!" She sniffed hard as she slipped her arms around Dad's waist. She wanted to stay forever in his arms.

"Listen to me, Tina." He held her away and lifted her chin so she'd have to look up at him. "I've been trying to tell you that I want to marry Mary."

Tina tried to jerk away but he held her firmly.

"I want you to love Mary. She'll make a wonderful mother for you. I love her, honey. I want you to try."

"Why should I? You love her. She loves you. That should be enough. Why should *I* matter?" Tina wanted to run from the house and keep running.

"Stop it! You are important to me. I love you, Tina. You're my precious daughter." His grip tightened on her arms. "But my life can't stop just because you want me all to yourself. Learn to love others, Tina. You've closed your heart against everyone since your mother died. I know you're afraid of being hurt again."

"Stop! Please, leave me alone!" The room

seemed to spin and Tina closed her eyes. "Just go to Mary and leave me alone."

"Grow up, Tina!" She looked up in surprise at the harsh tone of his voice. "You've been trying to prove to me that you're mature. Right now you are acting worse than a baby. Let me have a life of my own. I want to have Mary here with me. I need her, Tina. I love her very much."

Tina stood quietly, studying Steve's face. She did love him. She didn't want to hurt him. She sighed and touched the graying hair at his temples. "I'll try, Dad," she whispered. Oh, it was hard!

"Thank you, sweetheart." He hugged her, then set her free, a wide smile on his handsome face.

Tina managed a slight smile. "I have to get dinner on." The delicious aroma of the pot roast she'd put in the oven before church drifted into the hallway.

"I'm hungry. I'll help make the salad."

"Never mind, Dad. Just sit in your chair and read. Aunt Edith probably has the salad done." Tina hurried away. She didn't want Dad in the kitchen with Mary. It would be terrible to watch the love looks between them. She'd get sick if Dad said anything about marrying Mary, right in front of everyone.

In the kitchen Edith turned to Tina with a smile. "Everything is under control, Tina. You and Rita set the table." Edith pushed her hair away from her face. "I sent Mary in to change. I didn't want her to ruin that beautiful dress."

Tina watched the gravy bubble in the heavy skillet. She really was not needed and it made her feel left out. After all, the cooking and cleaning were to be her jobs until Mrs. Evans returned. She started for the dining room, then stopped. "Where did this come from?" It was a beautiful-looking strawberry pie.

"Mary made it special for Steve." Edith laughed. "You are a very lucky girl, Tina. It's not every day that a woman will even look at a man who has a teenage daughter."

Tina stiffened. She bit her lower lip to keep from saying something sharp. Finally she said, "I'll go set the table." She walked quickly to the dining room, then stopped.

Dad and Mary were standing near the window. They didn't see her and she wished that she hadn't seen them. He had both arms around Mary and they were kissing. Before she could run, Dad looked up and saw her. Her face felt on fire and her hands icy cold.

"Tina, Mary has just agreed to marry me."

"I love him, Tina," said Mary in her soft voice. "I want to make him a good wife. And I want to be a good mother to you."

Tina whirled around and ran back to the kitchen, her chest heaving, her eyes brimming with tears. How could Dad do this to her? How could he expect her to accept Mary as her *mother*!

SIX

A Visit
from Dallas

Tina frowned impatiently as Phil rode past at a gallop. He sure liked to show off his trick riding for Rita and Rob. Tina wanted to tell Rita to ignore Phil so he'd go away, but Rita liked him! She said she liked him better than the boy back home. Tina twisted her boot in the sand. Phil was all right as a friend to talk about horses or go fishing with. But a boy-friend?

"Look at that, Tina!" cried Rob, grabbing her arm as Phil clung to the saddle horn and flipped from one side of Ginger to the other. "I'd sure like to learn to do that!"

Rita frowned scornfully. "You can't even ride well yet, Rob. You'd get trampled if you tried that."

Tina stepped closer to Rob. "He could learn, Rita. It just takes a lot of practice." Tina could barely believe she was sticking up for Rob. The look of gratitude on his face brought a warm smile to her lips.

Phil pulled Ginger to a sliding stop. "Do you

want to show them what you can do, Tina?" He held out the reins to her. Tina wanted to reach for them, but stopped herself.

"Not today, Phil," she said stiffly.

"Can you really trick ride?" asked Rob, staring in awe at her. "I want to see."

"Tina's better than I am," said Phil, standing with one hand on his hip, the other holding the reins. "She taught me all I know." He smiled and she found herself smiling back. Teaching him had been a lot of fun.

Rita stepped close to Ginger, her hand on the saddle. "Let me ride, Phil."

When Phil eagerly agreed, Tina felt a sick feeling knife through her stomach. Why should she care that Phil liked Rita? It kept them both away from her when she wanted to be alone.

As a dusty blue car turned in the drive, Phil turned to Tina with a frown. "Looks like you're having company, Tina. Just don't get too friendly with Dallas."

"Mind your own business, Philip Rhyner!" Tina watched until the car parked outside the garage. Her heart leaped as Dallas stepped from the car. He was dressed in a blue tee shirt and jeans with blue and white tennis shoes. She wanted to look at him forever. She heard Rita tell Phil that they should ride away a while.

"Who's Dallas?" whispered Rob.

Tina flushed and looked at Rob. "I want to talk to him alone, OK? Don't hang around after I introduce you." She saw his face pale under his freckles and knew she'd embarrassed or hurt him. That was just too bad! She had to talk to Dallas alone.

A few minutes later she was alone with Dallas as they walked slowly toward the pond, and she didn't know how to act or what to say.

Finally they stopped and Dallas turned toward her. She saw his frown and was puzzled by it.

"What's wrong, Dallas?" she asked.

"Did I say something was wrong?" He rested his hands on his hips. "Do you think your dad will let me take you for a ride?"

Her heart sank. Frantically she searched for just the right thing to say. Her neck felt damp with perspiration. "I can't go anywhere today, Dallas. I have company."

He scratched his head. "That's too bad. I was going to let you drive my car."

She wiped her damp palms down her jeans. "We'll have to make it another time."

"I suppose we will." He turned abruptly toward the house. "I'm going to ask Steve if you can go to the show with me Saturday night."

Tina licked her dry lips. "I can't! I really can't go, Dallas. My cousins will still be here."

"We'll double-date. Rita and Phil, you and me."

Tina looked wildly toward the ranch house. What could she say to Dallas to keep him from talking to Dad? "Aunt Edith doesn't let Rita date yet," she said frantically.

Suddenly Dallas grasped her arms, and she looked in alarm at his angry face. He was hurting her and she tried to break free. His grip tightened.

"How old are you, Tina Lambert?"

Tina's heart dropped to her feet and her legs felt too weak to hold her. She cleared her throat. "How did you find out?"

"This morning after church, Tom Elders said something about you and we got to talking. When he said you were thirteen I almost fell over." He shook her roughly. "Why did you lie to me?"

Tears stung her eyes. "I was afraid you wouldn't ask me out if you knew my right age." She lifted her chin defiantly. "I look sixteen. I could pass for sixteen!"

"And I reckon Steve Lambert agreed to his little girl going out with me. I reckon!" He dropped his hands and she rubbed the painful spots. "That's why we couldn't meet here and then ride out to Tanner Hill, isn't it? Your daddy said you couldn't go with boys until you got older."

Anger surged through Tina. She stamped her booted foot, her eyes blazing. "I do as I please, Dallas Tromley! Nothing Dad says to me will stop me. If you don't want to take a chance, then fine! Just get in your car and get out of here. Who needs you anyway?" Tears stung her eyes but she ignored them. "I don't need a boyfriend who steals from old men!"

"Keep your voice down, Tina!" He looked around nervously. "Do you want someone to hear you?"

"I think I'll just go tell whoever will listen." She doubled her fists at her sides and stood with her boots apart. "Codge Farenholz happens to be my friend. I almost told him when he was here yesterday. Do you know that, Dallas Tromley? And I would have but I couldn't, because I love you."

He grabbed her hands and held them even when she tried to break free. "You have a crazy way of showing you care. How do you think I feel learning that my girl is only thirteen and isn't allowed to date?"

Tina stood perfectly still. "Am I your girl?"

"Sure you are."

"I am?" She could barely breathe as she stared up into his warm brown eyes.

"Do you think I would tell my secrets to just anyone?" He grinned and rested his hands on her shoulders.

"I . . . I guess not."

"And you won't tell Codge Farenholz, will you?"

She trembled and could hardly think with him so close. "I won't tell Codge."

"Or your dad?"

She shook her head.

"Is this a private conversation?" Phil stood just behind her, his hazel eyes snapping as he looked at Dallas's hands on Tina's shoulders.

Tina flushed and was relieved when Dallas dropped his hands. She did not want Phil to see how much she liked Dallas. She knew that was the only reason she didn't want him to see Dallas touch her. "What do you want, Phil? Did you decide to stop showing off to Rita?"

"Her mother called her in." Phil swatted a fly away from his curly blond hair. "She wanted you, too, so I said I'd get you."

"So you told her," said Dallas coldly. "Now you can go back to the barn or wherever you hang out."

Tina frowned at Dallas. She didn't like him saying mean things to Phil. After all Phil was her friend—had been for almost a year now.

"Let's go, Tina," said Phil softly. "It must be important if your aunt sent me to get you."

"She can walk to the house with me," snapped Dallas, catching Tina's hand in his.

Hastily Tina pulled free. "We'll all three walk to the house." She looked up at the boys and wondered why they were angry at each other. They had only met a couple of weeks ago.

Phil smiled at her. "I'll race you," he said, his hazel eyes twinkling.

Tina leaped forward with Phil beside her.

She had run only a short distance when suddenly she stopped. Her skin pricked with embarrassment. How could she act like such a little kid in front of Dallas?

SEVEN

Terrible News

Tina watched wistfully until the dust settled from Dallas's car. When would she see him again?

"He's not worth it, Tina." Phil tugged her hair gently. "Your aunt wants you, remember."

"You don't have to remind me," she said stiffly.

Phil pushed his hands into his pockets and hunched his shoulders. "I liked the other Tina better."

She stared up in surprise. What on earth did he mean? "What other Tina?"

"The one who laughs and plays with me and never snaps my head off."

She doubled her fists. "That Tina left the minute Dad got mixed up with those church people and Mary Lockwood."

"I'm one of those church people. Does that mean you hate me now?"

She frowned. She hadn't thought of Phil as one of them. She knew he was a Christian. But he was different. "I don't hate you, Phil."

She left him standing beside the garage. She would try not to snap at him.

Suddenly the screen door burst open and Rob rushed out, almost colliding with Tina.

"Guess what? Uncle Steve and Mary are going to get married next week so that we can be here for the wedding!"

Tina backed away, her hand at her mouth. Getting married next week? How could Dad do that to her?

"You're not gonna faint, are you, Tina?" asked Rob in concern.

Tina wheeled around and raced toward the barn. Ginger still stood at the corral, saddled. As she jerked the reins free Phil caught her arm and held her tightly.

"What's wrong, Tina?"

Violently Tina struck out, hitting Phil in the mouth. He staggered back and she leaped into the saddle.

Tears streamed down her face and the wind whipped her hair wildly. She heard the pounding hooves in her head over the words Rob had spoken. Dad and Mary. Dad and Mary! How could Dad get married again? He didn't need a wife. He had her.

Suddenly a dog barked nearby and Ginger reared, almost throwing Tina out of the saddle. Tina quieted Ginger, then noticed

Codge Farenholz standing beside the barbed wire fence that separated his property from Lamberts'. Jim Bridger barked again.

"Come lay down, Jim Bridger," commanded Codge gruffly. He tongued his chew of tobacco into his other cheek. "What's the hurry, Tina Lambert?"

She slipped from the saddle and stood across the fence from him, her hands locked together in front of her. "Dad is going to marry Mary Lockwood next week!"

Codge slapped his thigh with a broad grin. "That is mighty good news, little girl. Steve needs a woman around the house."

"What do you know about it? You don't have a woman around the house and you get along just fine."

"I got Jim Bridger here to keep me from getting lonely." He rested his work-roughened hand on the dog's multicolored head.

Tina lifted her chin. "And Dad has me!"

" 'Course he does, little girl. But Steve is young. He needs a wife."

"You don't care about how I feel. Nobody cares how I feel!" She swung around and leaped into the saddle, yelling to Ginger. She would not listen to another word Codge said. Oh, she hoped Dallas and his friends stole every bit of money Codge had sacked away.

Tina leaned low over the saddle and cried loud racking sobs until her throat ached. Why couldn't she die? Living hurt too much! It might have been better if she'd gone visiting with Mom, and been drowned with her. Living was too hard, too painful!

Finally Ginger slowed to a walk, then stopped completely at the cottonwood near Tanner Hill. Tina slipped from the saddle and dropped the reins. She knuckled the tears from her eyes. A black crow cawed and flew away. With a moan Tina sank to the grass under the tree. A mosquito buzzed around her head. How could she ever go back to the ranch and face everyone? She would not pretend that she was happy for Dad. She would never be nice to Mary!

In agitation Tina jumped to her feet and looked wildly around. Even in the wide open spaces she felt trapped, locked up in a small stall as Dad locked his favorite stallion. Was there a way out? She pressed her hands against her hot cheeks.

Ginger lifted her head and neighed. She bobbed her head up and down and neighed again.

Tina turned in alarm. Someone was coming, someone Ginger knew. Would Phil have ridden out after her?

With a running leap Tina landed in the saddle, scrambling for the reins. She turned and saw Dad on Colonel, riding hard toward her. Oh, she had to get away!

Wind whipped her hair back as Ginger

stretched into a run. Nobody ever outran Colonel, but this time she'd give it a try. What would she say to Dad if he caught her? How angry would he be?

Blood pounded in her ears, mixed with pounding hoofbeats. Was Dad catching up to her? How long could Ginger run at breakneck speed?

Suddenly a strong arm wrapped around Tina and lifted her from the saddle. She kicked the stirrups from her feet and was forced to release the reins. She was pulled unceremoniously against a hard chest. She turned her head and stared into Dad's set face. She was in for trouble now!

Steve dropped to the ground and gripped Tina's arms. "What were you trying to do—kill yourself? I could break you in two!"

Tears slid down Tina's hot cheeks, and she wanted to rest her head against Dad's chest until he soothed away her hurt.

"Dry those fake tears, Tina Ranea Lambert! We have some talking to do."

He shook her until her hair flipped into her face. "What made you ride that horse to death? She could've stepped in a hole. Were you trying to break your neck?"

Tina gulped and sniffed hard. "Rob told me," she whispered hoarsely. "Is it true?"

Steve took a deep breath and loosened his grip. "It is true. I'm sorry Rob told you. Mary and I wanted to. Phil told you to go to the house. We were going to make plans together."

"You don't need me to make plans," cried Tina, trying to break free. She winced as his grip tightened.

"I love you, Tina. I want you to be happy. Having a mother, especially one as kind and sweet as Mary, will be very good for you. Give her a chance, honey. She already loves you. Won't you at least try to accept Mary into the family?"

She wanted to scream no, but she could not hurt Dad that much. He did love her. He had ridden out to find her and talk to her. He really did care about her! "Daddy, I can't accept Mary. I don't know what's wrong with me. I promise myself that I'll try to be nice to her, then I just can't!"

"Oh, Tina." He pulled her close and he smelled like leather and sweat. "Honey. let God take care of your hurts. He loves you even more than I do. He'll take away all the agony and loneliness that you feel. He'll help you to love others the way I know you want to, deep in your heart."

Fresh tears spilled down her cheeks as she clung to him. Could God really do that for her? A strange yearning deep within her surprised and puzzled her. Would God fill the emptiness inside her if she asked him to? But why should God love *her*?

Steve wiped the tears from Tina's cheeks. Tenderly he kissed first one cheek, then the other. "You are precious to me, Tina. I love you. Let's go home and make plans together. It will be wonderful to be a complete family." He smiled and laugh lines spread from the corners of his blue eyes to his graying sideburns. "I need a wife, honey. I love Mary in the way a man was made to love a woman. My life is not complete without her. I want to be happy with Mary, but I can't be completely happy unless you are too. Will you try for me?"

She leaned her head against his broad chest. "I'll try, Daddy." It was easy to agree with him while leaning on him for strength. What would she do when she stood alone and Mary leaned on him?

"Let's go home." He whistled for Ginger as he reached for Colonel's reins.

Tina took a deep breath and slowly let it out. For Dad's sake she would try to get along with Mary.

Wearily Tina mounted Ginger. She looked at Dad and managed a weak smile. Side by side they rode to the ranch. Tina wanted to stay by his side and keep on riding.

EIGHT

The Wedding

Tina stood perfectly still in the little room at the back of the church, waiting for Aunt Edith to tell her it was time to walk down the aisle. Her hand tightened on the long stem of the dark pink rose. The fragrance seemed to fill the room. She caught her reflection in the full length mirror and wondered why the girl did not show the unhappiness she felt. The soft folds of the light pink dress almost touched the floor. Her long brown hair curled softly down her shoulders and back. What was she doing here? She should be in jeans and an old shirt, on Blaze's back, racing across the pasture with Dallas beside her.

The door opened and Tina saw a flutter of white in the mirror. Slowly she turned, her heart racing, to confront Mary Lockwood.

"You look beautiful, Tina," said Mary, her brown eyes shining with happiness. "I came in to tell you how glad I am that you agreed to stand up with us. You've been so helpful this past week." Mary walked closer, her gown swirling around her legs. "Thank you, Tina. You've helped make this a beautiful day that we won't forget."

Tina bit her lower lip. She didn't want Mary's thanks. Finally she managed to mumble something appropriate.

"Tina, I know this isn't easy for you. I think that once we get better acquainted, we'll get along well." Mary carefully pushed her veil away from her cheek. "I love Steve very much, Tina. I want to live with him, share my life with him always."

Tina wanted to run from the room. For just a second she felt a warmth toward Mary, then she pushed the feeling away. Mary was an intruder. Mary was wrecking her life.

"I was in love when I was eighteen, and the boy decided he wanted to marry someone else." Mary licked her lips. "I was hurt so badly that I said I would never fall in love again. But, Tina, Jesus healed all that pain. He made me free to love again. Today is the happiest day of my life. Can you try to share in my love and my happiness?"

Tina blinked away tears as she slowly nodded yes. If she couldn't have happiness for herself, then she would allow Dad and Mary to have a little.

Gently Mary touched Tina's cheek. "I am

very glad that Steve had you all these years. I'm glad that now I can share in your life."

Tina stared into Mary's face, searching for any sign of pretense. She seemed to mean every word. How would it feel to have a mother again?

The door opened and Edith walked in, smiling happily. "It's time, you two. Tina, you look beautiful." And suddenly Tina felt beautiful. She even managed a smile as Edith pulled Mary's veil over her face and arranged it around her shoulders.

"Here's your bouquet, Mary." Edith laid the long-stemmed roses in Mary's arms, then picked up her single rose. "You go first, Tina. I'll be right behind you."

Slowly Tina walked up the aisle. Tears pricked her eyes as Steve turned and watched her walk toward him. Jim Boyer and Slim Rhyner stood beside him, their eyes on the minister.

As Tina reached the altar Steve stepped out, took her arm and walked her to the spot where she was to stand. He kissed her. "I love you, honey," he whispered.

"I love you, Daddy." She smiled mistily as he walked back to his place. A hard lump settled in her throat at the expression on his face as Mary walked to meet him. Would anyone ever love her that way? Dallas had said she was his girl, but he didn't love her.

Abruptly she pushed that thought aside.

Dallas did love her. He would not say she was his girl if he didn't.

Was he in the church, watching her right at this minute? All the church people had been invited. Steve had asked several of his friends, including Codge Farenholz. Codge had said he'd never been in church before, and he didn't know if his system could stand the shock.

The words of the ceremony droned on and Tina moved restlessly. She saw Mary hand her bouquet to Aunt Edith. A band seemed to tighten around Tina's chest as the bride and groom exchanged rings.

Her entire life was changed. Suddenly she had both a mother and a father. Tina wanted to push Mary aside and tell her that there was no room for her in their lives, but she forced herself to stand still and watch as Steve lifted the veil and kissed Mary.

Tina watched as they rushed down the aisle away from her. She wanted to run after them and beg Dad not to forget her during his two-week honeymoon.

In a daze Tina took Slim Rhyner's arm and hurried after Edith and Jim Boyer. The wedding was over. Could she make it through picture-taking and the reception?

Later, as Tina lifted a glass of punch to her lips, Phil walked up with a grin. He tipped his head and studied her until she blushed.

"Is this the same girl who caught frogs with

me not long ago?" he asked in mock surprise. "Is this the same girl who can rope a steer and clean out a barn?"

Tina giggled, then stopped herself. "Leave me alone, Phil. Don't make it any worse than it already is."

He pulled out a chair and sat down beside her. "I was trying to make it easier, Tina." He leaned close to her. "Let's go fishing first thing in the morning. We haven't gone in a long time. We'll get up about four, pack a breakfast and go."

She twisted the glass in her hands. It did sound like fun. It would make tomorrow go faster. "Just make sure you set your alarm this time. I don't want to wake up the whole place just to get you up."

"Don't you worry, Tina. I'll be up at three just to get ready quicker. I wouldn't be late for anything."

Tina looked up to see Rita walking toward them. "I suppose you'll ask Rita to go with us."

"Not on your life! It'll be just you and me and the fish."

Tina leaned back with a satisfied smile.

"Here comes Dallas," said Phil sharply. "Don't go inviting him."

She was surprised that she didn't want to. "I won't," she murmured just as Rita and Dallas reached them.

"Hi," said Dallas with a warm smile. "You look very pretty today."

"Thank you." She wanted to hold out her hands and have him take them, but she would not do it with Phil looking on.

Rita tugged Phil away with her and Dallas sat beside Tina. "Will you stop looking at Phil Rhyner and look at me?" said Dallas sharply.

She frowned. "I hate the way Rita acts with Phil. She thinks he belongs to her."

"Let her have him. Who cares?"

Tina laughed self-consciously. She didn't care. If Phil was dumb enough to like Rita, then let him.

"Where are they going on their honeymoon?" asked Dallas as he looked across the room where Steve and Mary stood with Edith.

"To Hawaii." Tina locked her fingers together in her lap to stop their trembling. She and Dad were to have gone to Hawaii on vacation. Now, Dad wouldn't have time.

"That takes a lot of money."

Tina frowned. Why did Dallas always have to bring up money?

"Look over there." Dallas motioned with his head.

Tina saw Codge Farenholz walk across the room to shake hands with Steve. Tina chuckled. Codge was dressed in brand new jeans and a blue shirt. His old boots were shined and clean. He clutched his shabby Stetson in his hands. The white hair around the back of his head and above his ears looked newly cut. "I'm going over to talk to him, Dallas." She started to move and he grabbed her arm.

"What are you going to say to him, Tina?"

"I just want to tell him that I'm glad he came." She frowned impatiently.

"Just remember your promise!"

She twisted her arm free. "I remember," she whispered hoarsely.

He pushed his chair back and stood up. "I might be over tomorrow. We can have a nice long talk all alone if you can keep that Phil Rhyner away."

Tina stared after Dallas as he strode across to the door and out. He could be terrible at times. She sighed. He could be wonderful too.

Slowly Tina walked across the room toward Codge Farenholz. He looked different without Jim Bridger beside him.

"Hi, Codge."

He smiled. "Howdy, little girl. You look good enough to eat."

"Thank you. I'd be as tough as your old boots if you tried."

He chuckled. "You would be at that." He nodded to the door. "Walk me out of here, Tina. I don't know as I can make it. All this godliness is beginning to wear on me."

She knew just what he meant. The people at church seemed so nice. It would be very easy to give in and accept them—and Jesus. Tina shook her head. What was she thinking of? She squared her shoulders and walked Codge across the room to the door.

NINE

Eavesdropping

Tina proudly held up the string of trout. The early morning breeze blew against her. She moved her head and the ponytails over her ears bobbed. "Oh, Phil! This is our best catch yet!"

"It was fun, wasn't it?" He grinned at her as he pulled apart his fly rod and slipped it into the brown cotton case.

"It's peaceful here, Phil." She looked at the clear blue stream and remembered the years of pleasure it had given her. She lowered the stringer into the cold water and hooked it securely. "I could camp right here the rest of my life."

Phil sat beside a rock and opened the knapsack of food. "I could too, Tina."

She sat beside him and reached for a thick ham sandwich. Her stomach cramped with hunger and she bit eagerly into the home-made bread.

Phil dug into the bag and pulled out a jar of dill pickles. "Look what I brought."

She giggled and shook her head. "Dill pickles for breakfast?"

"I knew you loved them with ham sandwiches."

For some strange reason tears pricked her eyes. She had forgotten how kind he could be. "Thank you, Phil."

"Hey, don't cry," he said softly. "It's only a jar of pickles."

"I know. It's just that you haven't done anything for me in a long time."

"Because you wouldn't let me, Tina."

She sighed. "I know. I seem to be living inside this dark gloomy cloud, and no matter how hard I try, I can't get out."

"I'm very sorry, Tina. I'd like to help you."

She shook her head. "You can't, Phil. Nobody can." She held up her hand as he started to speak. "Don't say anything about God to me. I don't want my beautiful morning ruined."

He sighed as he pulled his sandwich out of the plastic bag. "I wouldn't ruin the morning for you, Tina." He smiled and his teeth looked pearly white against his sun-browned face. "I want this morning to be perfect for both of us. I've missed you, Tina. I sure don't like fishing alone. You are my very best friend and I'm glad to have you here with me."

Tina smiled as she remembered Phil's

uncle saying Phil could charm a filly into doing anything he wanted her to. Was he using that charm on her right now?

She ate two sandwiches, half a jar of pickles, and a large cinnamon roll. A cup of cold milk washed it all down. She sat back with a sigh, knowing they had to leave soon to do morning chores.

"Before we leave, I have to say something even if you get mad, Tina." She stiffened at his serious tone.

"What is it?" she asked sharply, her blue eyes holding his troubled gaze.

"This is not easy." He took a deep breath. "Watch out for Dallas Tromley. There's something about him that hits me wrong."

Tina pressed her arms tightly against herself. "What do you mean?"

"I don't know. I just know he means trouble for someone, and I don't want you to be that someone."

Did Phil know that she'd sneaked out with Dallas? Was he trying to tell her he knew? "Dallas wouldn't hurt me. He likes me." She'd wanted to say love but the word would not leave her tongue.

"Of course he likes you. You're pretty and fun to be with."

"He trusts me, Phil. He treats me like I'm grown up, not like a little kid."

Phil picked up a twig and snapped it loudly. "I hate to say this, Tina, but thirteen is not grown up. Thirteen shouldn't be grown up. Have fun while you are thirteen, like a thirteen-year-old. When you're sixteen, have fun as a sixteen-year-old."

She stiffened. Had he heard about her lie to Dallas? Who would tell him?

"Steve asked me to keep an eye on you while he was gone." Phil pushed his fingers through his blond curls. "And I said I would, especially when Dallas is around."

Tina leaped to her feet, her eyes blazing. "Why do you say that? Doesn't Dad trust me? What do you think I'll do?"

Phil jumped to his feet and stood beside her, his hands on his hips. "I know you, Tina. I know you like Dallas too much. Steve doesn't want you to go with guys, but I know if you had a half a chance you'd sneak out with Dallas."

"And you'd run off to Daddy and tell him everything, wouldn't you, big mouth? You would love it if you could make sure Dallas never came around."

"He makes me mad, Tina. He acts so big! He walks around like he owns the world. If he'd spend as much energy helping his mother fix up the old Tooker place as he does running with those friends of his, he could make something of himself and his home."

Tina gripped her hands together. Dallas had told her he hadn't seen Carl and Larry in a long time. She lifted her rounded chin. "I'm going home, Phil. It's too bad you had to ruin our morning."

He caught her arm and tried again to make her listen to him, but she jerked free.

"Do I tell you to stay away from Rita because she's bad for you?" snapped Tina.

"Rita is a nice girl. I like her."

"Nice! Rita doesn't know the meaning of the word."

"If you'd try a little, you'd learn to like your cousin."

"Do you think it's my fault that we don't get along? She hates me! She doesn't want to be friends."

"Easy, Tina. You're going to scream yourself hoarse."

She stamped her foot. "I'm getting out of here. Next time you want to go fishing, go with Rita!" Tina dashed to the horses. She jerked Blaze's cinch strap tight, then leaped into the saddle.

"You forgot the fish."

"You take them! I couldn't eat them!" She glared down at him. "And don't you ever give me another dill pickle!"

"I won't need to. You're sour enough already."

Her skin burned as she shouted to Blaze to run. She would not talk to Phil again as long as she lived, and when she did she'd be as nasty as possible!

By the time she finished her chores outdoors her anger was gone. She walked into the house wearily. Today she had to start cleaning Dad's bedroom. Aunt Edith was going to redecorate it while Dad was gone.

"Where have you been?" asked Rob as he jumped up from watching TV. "I wanted to help with chores."

"You don't know how," she snapped.

"I could try." He stood tall and looked her right in the eyes. "I want to learn all about ranch work. I'm going to have a ranch of my own someday just like this one."

Tina softened. "Sorry I snapped, Rob. Sure, I'll help you learn all you can. You'll be a lot of help."

He grinned as he tugged his tee shirt down over his tan shorts. "Where can I start?"

"I'm done outside for now but tonight you can help me."

"I don't want to watch TV all day. I want something to do."

"Where's Rita?"

He made a face. "Still in bed. Mom's cleaning the kitchen. She didn't want my help either."

"I could use a strong back for a while." She saw him puff up with pride and it made her feel good to know she was helping him. "I need to move the furniture out of Dad's room. Want to help?"

"Sure." He walked beside her down the hall to Steve's bedroom.

She took a deep breath and steeled herself, then stepped into the large room. She was glad Rob was beside her or she would have cried and run. With forced effort she pushed thoughts of Dad and Mary away and concentrated on telling Rob what had to be done.

Having Rob working beside her the rest of the day helped more than she thought possible. He even made her laugh a few times. To her surprise she enjoyed working with him, listening to his thoughts and interests. When had Rob changed? He'd once been a bratty little kid who followed her around, teasing and making trouble. But then, he had never been to visit more than two days at a time. Maybe she'd been wrong about him.

During night chores Rob stopped in the barn and looked at Tina. "I like you, Tina. You're fun to work with."

A warm feeling surged through her and she smiled at Rob. "I like you, too." Wow! She had never said that to him. And she realized with surprise that she did like him. It would be nice to have him around all the time.

"I like Phil, too. He's as nice as you are."

Tina grabbed a brush and walked to Blaze. Phil could be nice part of the time, but not to her—not ever again! "Do you want to brush Colonel, or not?" She wanted to bite her tongue for snapping at Rob. She saw the hurt look on his face, but she could not bring herself to apologize. Frantically she searched her mind for something nice to say to him to take away the tears he was fighting to hold back. "Tomorrow after my work is done I'll teach you the leaping mount, Rob."

His face brightened at once. "I can't wait! Can't we start right now? It stays light out for a long time."

Tina laughed. She had always been that eager to learn any new trick. "Not tonight, Rob. Tomorrow. I promise."

Later, in her bedroom, Tina thought of all the things she could teach Rob and how interested he would be to learn. She slipped on her bathrobe over her yellow nightgown. Her bare toes stuck out of the soft folds. She frowned, wondering where Rita had gone. She'd disappeared soon after supper and Tina hadn't seen her since.

Slowly Tina brushed her hair, then braided it in two braids that hung down her slender shoulders. She looked in the mirror and made a face. Now, she looked thirteen. She was glad Dallas couldn't see her.

She turned at a light tap on her door. "Come in." She waited, then smiled as Rob slipped into her room and quickly closed the door. His red hair seemed to stand on end and his green eyes were full of mischief.

"How would you like to hear something interesting?" he asked with a wide grin. The freckles stood out on his face and arms.

"What is it?" She knew he was excited.

"Rita and Phil are sitting right outside on the porch step and talking. I just happened to be kneeling in front of my window and I could see them and hear every word they said." He reached for the doorknob. "Want to come listen and watch? It'll be fun."

A cold knot settled in Tina's stomach. Of course Rita would be with Phil. She always was, every chance she had! It would serve him right if she and Rob eavesdropped. "Sure. I think that would be fun." But why didn't she feel like laughing? If he kissed Rita, she would be sick! He didn't like her that much, did he?

Silently Tina knelt in front of the open window beside Rob. Fragrance of the roses beside the house drifted into the room. Tina shivered. What would Phil want to say to Rita that took so long?

Tina listened as Rita asked Phil to explain once again why he was a Christian.

Rob nudged her and grinned. She knew he was thinking that Rita was faking her interest.

As Phil talked, Tina grew restless, almost panicky. She did not want to hear about Phil's parents being killed and Phil having no one until Slim Rhyner brought him to the ranch. Slim had taken him to church and taught him about God.

"I was empty inside," said Phil. "I was brokenhearted. I knew that I couldn't live all my life with those feelings. When Jesus took them away, I was happy again. I want to be like

Jesus, Rita. I want to learn more and more about him. He loves me! I think that was what made me turn to him for help. He loved me and knew all about me."

Tina locked her fingers tightly together and swayed back and forth. She felt that same yearning inside, a sad aching for something that she couldn't put her finger on. Could anyone love her like that—even Jesus?

"I want to be a Christian too, Phil," said Rita.

Tina gasped and jumped to her feet. She would not listen to another word! Rob tried to catch her arm but she brushed past him, not caring if she made noise or not.

She flung herself on her bed and sobbed against her pillow.

• TEN •

Abandoned Mine

Tina slipped behind the shed until Phil walked out of sight in the direction of the training corral. This morning she didn't want to talk to Phil. It had been bad enough to have Rita carrying on and on about how happy she was to be a believer. Even Rob had listened eagerly, almost yearningly. Tina had left when he'd asked Rita to pray with him.

Tina made a face as she walked toward the barn. Even Aunt Edith had been happy for Rita, had even agreed that she needed Jesus as her Savior too. Being at the breakfast table had been as bad as being in church! A dull ache in her heart made tears prick her eyes. Why was she feeling this way? Was she envious of their happiness?

Rob stepped out from behind the barn door, then laughed as Tina jumped in alarm.

"Are you going to teach me a trick now?"

Tina frowned. "I will when I get good and ready." She wanted to slap Rob's face and knock off that knowing grin. "I can't play around all day like you and that sister of yours do."

Rob's smile vanished and he pushed his hands deep into his pockets. His face flushed red. "I thought I was helping you, Tina. I thought you liked me."

A lump settled in her throat and she ignored it. With a toss of her head she walked past him. "I can change my mind, you know. You should know a city kid is never any help."

He ran after her and grabbed her arm. "Please, don't be mean to me again, Tina. You promised to teach me trick riding."

"Don't be such a baby, Rob! Go ask Phil."

"Ask me what?"

Tina spun around, her face red. She had thought he was gone for at least an hour. "Rob wants to learn some trick riding. I told him to ask you to teach him."

Phil clamped his hand on Rob's thin shoulder. "I will, Rob, but not today." Phil looked at Tina with a wide grin. "We have something exciting planned for today."

Tina frowned. Whom did he mean by "we"? "What's so exciting about cleaning out the horse barn?"

"We're going exploring at Tanner Hill today. You'll like that, Rob. Your mother said we could take a picnic and stay the day."

"Who planned it?" asked Tina with a scowl.

"Rita and I," answered Phil.

A pang of jealousy shot through her, making her glare angrily at Phil. "And who said you could have the day off?" She was glad to see his flush of embarrassment. "Or are you being paid to take the city cousins on an outing?"

Phil clenched his fists. "I know what you're doing, Tina, and you won't get away with it! We are going on a picnic at Tanner Hill. If you want to stay home and clean the barn, then stay home!"

Tina wanted to fly at him and hit him but she didn't dare. Phil would not allow her to do that. He was very strong. "Do you want me to go with you?"

"Sure we do," said Rob eagerly.

"I don't want you to if you're going to be ornery. It's up to you, Tina. We can get along without you."

Tina pushed her trembling hands into her jeans pockets before Phil could see how close she was to hitting him. "I'll go. But only to keep my cousins from being hurt in the mine."

"And because you can't stand to think of us at Tanner Hill having fun while you're slaving away here," said Phil, his hazel eyes boring into hers. "Don't think you fool me at all, Tina Ranea Lambert!"

Tina ran to the house before she burst with anger. She would fix him somehow! He'd be very sorry for talking to her that way!

"Did Phil find you, Tina?" asked Rita, looking up from the sandwiches she was fixing.

"He found me."

"It's going to be fun."

"Yeah, sure."

"Don't you want to go, Tina?" asked Edith as she set a jug of iced punch on the counter.

Tina shrugged. "I'll get the flashlights." She rushed away before they could say more. She did not want to go, but she did not want to stay home and let Rita spend all day with Phil. She'd make sure they didn't have any fun! Suddenly Tina stopped, a wicked smile on her lips. "I know what I can do!"

Quickly she walked into the study and closed the door. She picked up the phone and dialed Tromley's number, hoping that Dallas would answer. When he did she quickly explained that she wanted him to meet her at Tanner Hill for a picnic.

"I was forced to have my cousins join us," she said. "And Phil will come too, for Rita."

"We'll sneak away by ourselves, Tina."

Shivers of excitement ran up and down Tina's spine. "All right. Bring a flashlight, Dallas. This time we'll explore the mine."

After she hung up, Tina leaned against the desk, staring dreamily out the window. She remembered being close to Dallas. Would he kiss her again? It would serve Phil right if Dallas kissed her right in front of him!

While she helped with the lunch and later saddled up, Tina kept a smile on her face. She spoke kindly to Rita and Rob.

Phil walked up beside her as they led the horses into the yard. "You're up to something, Tina. I'd sure like to know what it is."

Her eyes widened in surprise. She kept her face turned from him so he couldn't see her expression. "You don't know what you're talking about, Phil. I'm happy about going today, that's all."

"I don't believe you, little girl."

She jerked around, glaring at him. "Don't call me that! I am not a little girl!"

"So you keep saying. Maybe someday I'll believe you."

She bit her tongue to keep from yelling at him. When he walked over to Rita to help her mount, Tina took a deep breath to calm herself. She would not let Phil make her mad. Soon she'd see Dallas. He wouldn't say bad things to her. And he would never call her a little girl.

Tina urged Blaze ahead of the others. She did not want to listen to Rita and Rob talking about how wonderful it was to be a Christian. Phil was telling them about reading the Bible and praying. She did not need to hear that from Phil today.

The sun burned against her head and

shoulders. A meadowlark warbled nearby, then flew away. This could have been a beautiful day. Tina moved restlessly in her saddle. What was wrong with her? She looked over her shoulder, then quickly forward again. How would it feel to ride together with Rob, Rita, and Phil and talk excitedly about God? Would she always be such an outsider? God didn't care about her. No one did!

The closer they rode to Tanner Hill, the more nervous Tina grew. Why had she called Dallas? Phil would be angry. He would tell Dad. She would have to act surprised to see Dallas and ask him to join them for the day. Phil must never know they'd arranged it ahead of time.

Tina smiled and relaxed.

"Someone is there," said Rita as she pointed to the horse in the shade of the cottonwood.

Tina urged Blaze into a run. She pulled him up short beside Molly and slid from the saddle.

"Dallas!"

"I'm here." He laughed as she jumped.

She looked up at him and her knees grew weak. Was he really that good-looking? She'd forgotten. "Dallas," she said breathlessly. "I have to tell the others that since you are here we should invite you to join us. They mustn't know that I called you."

He shrugged. "I'll go along with that." He

touched her cheek softly. "I missed you. Did you miss me?"

She nodded, then stepped back as the others rode up. "Look who's here! We have enough food for him to join us, don't we, Rita?" Tina looked quickly at Phil, then at Rita.

"I'm glad you're here, Dallas," said Rita with a wide smile. She pushed her auburn hair out of her face. "Do you like chicken sandwiches?"

"I like anything." He spoke to Rob, and Tina peeked again at Phil. She could tell he was steaming inside.

"We're going exploring," said Rob as he clicked his flashlight off and on.

"I came prepared for the same thing," said Dallas. "I've been wanting to go into the mine for a while now. It's not a place I'd want to walk into alone."

A few minutes later they crawled one by one through the boards into the mine shaft. Tina wrinkled her nose at the musty, closed-in smell. She stepped closer to Dallas.

"It's spooky in here," said Rob softly as he moved his light around.

"I hear something," whispered Rita. "What's in here?"

"A few rats," said Phil. "Don't be afraid. I'm right here with you. Give me your hand."

Tina wanted to shove Rita away from Phil. Instead, she said, "Oh, Dallas! Take my hand.

I'm scared." As his hand closed around hers she suddenly wished Phil was beside her and Dallas with Rita. But that was foolish. She loved Dallas!

"Who's going first?" asked Rob, his voice strained.

"We'll go first," said Dallas. "Stay right behind us, Rob."

Rita sneezed and said something about the dust. Tina caught a hanging bat with her beam of light. She shuddered. She would not want a bat in her hair.

"See the way the miners shored up the sides," said Phil, flashing his light around. He showed them an area where they probably found gold, and Rob wanted to chip away dirt and hunt in case they missed a little of the gold.

After they'd walked a way Rita asked how far back the tunnel went.

"I don't know," answered Phil. "I've been a long way back, then got scared of a cave-in, and came back out. Some mines went right through a hill to the other side. I don't know if this one does."

Tina had heard it might but she'd never checked it out. She didn't want to. Being inside a hill this far sent chills up and down her back.

"Let's go back," said Phil. "We've come far enough."

"Scared a little?" asked Dallas scornfully.

"Let's go back," said Phil sharply.

Suddenly Dallas stumbled and Tina toppled to the ground with him. She sneezed at the rising dust.

"I fell over something," said Dallas. "It feels like a person!"

Tina gasped and pointed her light down. "It is someone! Is he . . . dead?"

"I think so," said Dallas.

"I want out of here," wailed Rita.

"Let me see," said Phil as he knelt down beside Tina. She felt better with him close beside her.

"Can you see?" asked Rob hoarsely.

"He's already cold," said Dallas. "He must have been dead a long time."

Tina clutched Phil's arm. "Let's get out of here!"

"Wait!" Phil shone the light directly on the body's face. "What in the world?"

Suddenly Dallas burst out laughing. "It's a store dummy. I thought it would give you a thrill."

Tina gasped as Rita asked angrily if Dallas had actually put it there to scare them.

"I wanted you always to remember your trip into the mine," said Dallas, laughing again.

"We won't forget," said Rob sharply. "I'm getting out of here."

Tina waited impatiently for the others to start walking. She started to follow Dallas but Phil grabbed her arm.

He waited until the others were a few feet away, then he whispered, "So, you told him to come here today! And you wanted us to think he just happened to be here."

"Let go of me," whispered Tina, trying to jerk free. His grip tightened. "I wanted him to come today. What of it? You don't care. You have Rita!"

"And she's ten times better than you! She wouldn't fall for a guy with a warped mind."

"She fell for you, didn't she?"

He flung her arm from him. "Follow the others before I beat the tar out of you!"

She stumbled, then hurried toward the bobbing lights ahead, tears stinging her eyes.

ELEVEN

The Circle
of Love

The corners of Tina's wide mouth drooped as she watched Steve and Mary laughing and talking as they walked across the yard. They had been home a week already and Tina still had not talked to Dad alone.

"He doesn't care about me," she whispered as she leaned against the porch step. Who did care about her? Phil had not talked to her since the day in the mine except about ranch work. Once she'd suggested they go fishing again but he'd refused. Rob spent most of his time learning to spring from one side of the running horse to the other. Rita followed Phil everywhere. She only talked to Tina at night before they fell asleep, and then only about what she'd read in her Bible.

Tina rested her elbows on her knees and cupped her chin in her hands. Dallas had called only once in the past three weeks. He had said he'd been very busy. She'd seen him at church with his mother, but hadn't been able to talk to him. Once she'd seen him downtown talking with Carl Spence and Larry Postma. She had waved but Dallas had frowned. He couldn't still be planning to rob Codge. He had said he'd talk to her about it first to give her a chance to change his mind.

Tina moved restlessly. Thunder rumbled in the distance. Maybe the weather was making her feel strange. An ant crawled across her bare foot and she flicked it away.

"Steve. Steve." Edith hurried from the back door, the screen door slamming loudly.

Tina watched her dad stop and turn. His arm was around Mary and Tina closed her eyes so she couldn't see.

"What is it, Edith?" asked Steve. "I hope nothing is wrong."

"Harold just called. He's home! I'm going to pack and leave as soon as possible."

"I'll help you," said Mary. "I know how much you've missed Harold."

Edith laughed. "I just wish it wouldn't take so many hours to drive."

Tina's eyes flew open. How could she stay away from Mary with Rob, Rita, and Aunt Edith gone? How could she sit at the table with only Mary and Dad at every meal? What would Rob do if he couldn't practice riding every day?

Tina pulled her tee shirt down over her shorts. She really should offer to help Rita pack.

Rita was clicking open her suitcase as Tina walked into the bedroom.

"I just heard the news," said Tina stiffly. "I'll help you if you want. I know you're anxious to see your dad."

"I want to go home, but I want to stay here, too." Rita hugged a bundle of clothes, tears sparkling in her eyes. "I'll miss Phil. I wonder if he would write to me if I wrote to him."

Tina stiffened. "Phil's pretty busy."

"Not too busy for me."

Tina grabbed Rita's dresses off the hangers. "What about that boy back home? Don't you want him back?"

Rita frowned. "I forgot about him."

"You might as well forget about Phil. This year in school he'll have at least a dozen girl friends." A sharp pain shot through her at the thought. "He never sticks to one girl for long." Did Rita know that Phil didn't really have any girl friends, that he didn't date yet?

Rita studied Tina thoughtfully. "I don't understand why you don't like Phil. He likes you a lot. I can tell."

Tina stood perfectly still, a dress clutched in her hands. "He did like me, but not any more."

"You might be right." Rita folded her clothes and packed them neatly. "You haven't told me much about Dallas lately. Have you ridden with him since we were at Tanner Hill together?"

Tina hesitated. "No. I don't know if he likes me now."

"Do you still like him?"

"Of course!" She felt sure she did. She couldn't be in love one minute and out of love the next, could she?

Several minutes later Tina stood beside her aunt's car and watched as everyone hugged and kissed everyone else. Phil stood beside Rita, talking softly to her, too softly for Tina to hear. Didn't anyone notice that she was standing by herself all alone? Would it always be like this, this being outside the circle of love? Would the circle burst if she stepped into it? Tina frowned. What was she thinking? If she stepped into the circle of love, she'd be admitting that Mary was part of her family. Mary would never be her mother. Never!

Edith walked to Tina and pulled her close. She smelled like roses. "Tina, I enjoyed being here with you. You're a precious girl. Try to enjoy having a mother again. Mary is trying to win your love. Make your dad happy by learning to love her."

Tina pulled away. "Have a good trip, Aunt Edith. Say hello to Uncle Harold for me."

"I will." She kissed Tina's cheek. "I love you, honey."

Tina blinked back tears. She wanted to tell her aunt that she loved her but she was afraid she'd burst out crying. Numbly she told Rob and Rita goodbye. When Phil stepped up beside her, she wanted to hold his hand tightly. Tina had thought she'd be happy to see the cousins leave. But now she knew she would be very lonely without them. She'd gotten used to having them around. She looked up at Phil but he was looking at Rita. Tina bit her lower lip and forced her tears away.

Finally the car pulled out of the driveway and disappeared on the road. Tina could not move. She looked at Phil. Without a smile or a word he turned around and strode toward his uncle's house. Slowly Tina walked toward her house. Dad and Mary walked just ahead of her with their arms around each other's waists. Who was around to help her over this lonely time? Who cared enough to see that she felt bad for not being nice to Rob and Rita? Phil must know. He always knew how she felt and what she thought. Was he so hurt by Rita's leaving that he couldn't think about her?

Mary looked back, then stopped and smiled at Tina. "Things will be very quiet around here now, Tina. We'll have a chance to get to know one another."

Tina wanted to walk up to Mary and slip her arm in hers, but she just couldn't.

"Mrs. Evans called a while ago, Tina," said Steve. "She said she can't come back to work for us. Mary said she doesn't mind."

"We'll be a real family with the three of us," said Mary softly. "I'll like that."

"I want Mrs. Evans back," said Tina sharply. She saw the pain in Mary's eyes, and wanted to take back the words. Tina really didn't care if Mrs. Evans came back, but she couldn't stand to think of all the hours she'd spend alone with Mary. Finally she shrugged. "Oh, well. I can cook almost as good as Mrs. Evans."

"I'll be doing the cooking, Tina," said Mary firmly. "You have too much to do already."

Tina just stared at her. Should she be glad or angry? Finally she rushed into the house to her bedroom. She slammed the door and flung herself across her bed. Life was going to be very different now. Would Dad and Mary be happier if she left? They didn't really need her around. She could go live with Aunt Edith until she was old enough to be on her own. But she wouldn't ever see Dallas if she did that.

With her blue eyes wide Tina sat up. She would call Dallas and ask him to meet her in the west pasture for a long ride. That would take away all the strange feelings she had.

She quietly stepped into the hall and listened. Dad and Mary were in the kitchen. With a sigh of relief she hurried to the study and closed the door behind her. Dallas had to be home!

She sank weakly to a chair when she heard his voice.

"Could you meet me today for a ride,

Dallas?" She closed her eyes and saw his warm brown eyes smiling down at her.

"I can't today, Tina."

Her eyes snapped open and she leaned forward. "Why not?"

"I have plans, important plans."

Her stomach cramped. "What plans, Dallas?"

"Don't ask, Tina, and you won't worry. I can't talk now."

"Please, don't hang up yet." She gripped the receiver and her face turned pale. "You aren't going to rob Codge, are you?"

"I knew I shouldn't have told you about that! Forget it, will you? What you don't know can't hurt you."

"Don't do it, Dallas. You might hurt Codge. You might get hurt yourself!"

"Codge isn't home. I won't get hurt. If you really love me, Tina, you won't tell anyone what's happening."

She tried to talk but the phone clicked on his end. A buzzing filled her ears and she numbly replaced the receiver, then just stared at it. What could she do?

Just then the door opened and Mary walked in. "Oh, Tina. I'm sorry. I didn't know you were in here." She walked closer. "Tina! What's wrong? Oh, honey, what has hurt you so much?"

Tina lifted her face and tears slipped down

her cheeks. She reached for Mary's hand but found herself wrapped in Mary's arms with her head on Mary's breast.

"I'm here, Tina. You don't have to be alone with your problem. I love you. I want to help you."

Thankfully Tina clung to her, glad for the comfort. Finally she pulled away and stood unsteadily to her feet.

"You are not alone, Tina. I'm here to help you. Your father will help you. Share that burden you are carrying."

Tina locked her fingers together tightly. "I can't, Mary," she whispered. "I just can't!"

Slowly Tina walked back to her room. What could she do to stop Dallas and his friends? Her brain seemed to be empty of any thoughts. She leaned against her closed door and pressed her fingers to her temples. Dallas was going to rob Codge Farenholz and there was nothing she could do to stop him.

TWELVE

Codge
Farenholz

Restlessly Tina paced her bedroom. Twice she'd reached for the doorknob to tell Dad about Dallas's plans. Reluctantly she had to admit to herself that part of the reason she couldn't tell was so Dad would not learn about how she'd sneaked out with Dallas.

In desperation Tina rushed from her room, calling to Dad that she was going for a short ride on Blaze. Before the door slammed behind her, she heard him warn her to watch the weather.

Thunder cracked and Tina jumped. She looked up at the overcast sky. The storm seemed a long way off yet.

Phil stopped at the corral fence as she saddled Blaze. Tina suddenly felt all thumbs. She could feel his eyes on her, boring into her back as she worked. Finally she whipped around to yell for him to go away, then closed her mouth. He was already walking toward two of the ranch hands beside the tool shed.

Tina frowned angrily. If Phil didn't want to talk to her, then she sure wouldn't talk to him. Wind swirled sand around her feet and blew back her long brown hair. Impatiently she leaped into the saddle and rode out of the yard. She would not bother with Phil.

She rode until she could think a little better. Once she stopped to watch a small herd of antelope. Thunder cracked louder and she knew it was coming closer. She took a deep breath as Blaze walked around a cactus.

"I have to do something. I can't let them rob Codge!" She urged Blaze into a run. She'd tell Dad and he'd drive right over to Codge's place. Oh, it was great to know that Codge was away until late that night. At least he wouldn't be harmed by the boys.

Just as Tina rode into the yard a faded red flatbed truck pulled out of the driveway. Her heart sank as she stood in the stirrups. Codge was heading home! He had not stayed away as he'd planned! She had to stop him before he reached home! Maybe she could catch him at his lane if she rode across country.

She caught sight of Phil leading Ginger into the yard. Phil would help her.

She stopped beside him, dust rising up to choke her. "Phil, we've got to stop Codge. It's important." She saw the surprise on his face but he didn't ask questions. He leaped into the saddle and turned with Tina across country.

Codge could not beat them. At top speed, his old truck barely moved. Thunder cracked almost overhead and Tina groaned. The storm must not hit before they could reach Codge.

"God if you really care for us, help me stop Codge from getting hurt," whispered Tina urgently as she leaned low in the saddle.

Codge's old silver mailbox was a beautiful sight to Tina. She stopped Blaze as Phil pulled up Ginger.

"Look, Tina." Phil pointed to a cloud of dust farther down the lane. "Codge is up there. We didn't beat him. What's so urgent?"

"Some boys are going to rob him. We must stop them!" She leaned forward, calling to Blaze.

Hoofbeats thundered in her ears. Her breast rose and fell with the wild beating of her heart. Her lips felt cracked and dry. From the corner of her eye she saw the blur of Phil on Ginger. What was Phil thinking? Would he guess one of the boys was Dallas?

The old truck sat near a sagging shed when Tina pulled Blaze to a stop. Frantically she looked around. Codge was not in sight. Where was Jim Bridger? He should be barking. Oh, Dallas wouldn't kill Jim Bridger, would he? Tears stung her eyes and she turned helplessly to Phil.

"Codge!" shouted Phil, his head up, his back straight. "Codge, where are you?"

Tina shivered and she gripped the reins tighter. Should they dismount and look around for Codge? He couldn't have gotten very far.

Just then the wiry old man walked from around the shed, his hand on his dog's head. He pushed his battered hat back and stared up at Tina and Phil. "What's all the yelling about? And what do you mean by riding hard behind me? I thought you were a couple of thieves after me."

Tina looked quickly around. Had Dallas come and gone already? She moved restlessly. "Did you see a sign of anyone here?"

The old man's eyes narrowed as he stepped closer to Blaze. "What're you trying to tell me, little girl?"

She slipped to the ground, her legs suddenly weak. "I heard someone was going to rob you, Codge. We'll look around with you to see if anyone has."

"If anyone's been here, Jim Bridger will know it." Codge walked toward his weathered house that looked to Tina like a shack. She had asked him once why he didn't build himself a more comfortable house, but he'd said he liked how he lived.

Tina moved close to Phil as they walked with Codge. Shivers ran up and down her spine. She watched Jim Bridger. If anyone was around, the dog's hair would stand on end and he'd growl deep in his throat.

"Are you sure someone was planning to rob Codge?" asked Phil, looking down at Tina. "Maybe somebody was pulling your leg."

If only that were true! "I'm sure someone was planning it."

A few minutes later Codge shook his head. "Nobody's been here. I'm glad you're concerned about me, little girl, but I think somebody was just talking. Nobody's tried robbing me since Jim Bridger here practically tore off that polecat's leg."

Tina locked her fingers together. "Just be very careful, Codge. Keep both ears open."

"Where did you hear the story, Tina?" asked Phil.

She twisted her boot in the sand, her eyes on the dusty toe of her boot. "I just heard."

"From Dallas?"

Tina looked up with a gasp. "Why do you say that?"

"I know he's been planning something. Was it Dallas?"

Numbly she nodded.

"That's the boy who lives at the Tooker place?" asked Codge.

"Yes," said Phil sharply. "And Tina fell for him!"

"I did not!" Her whole body felt on fire and she knew her face was bright red. "I couldn't help it! He treated me like a grown up, not the little girl you think I am."

Suddenly Jim Bridger growled deep in his

throat. Tina saw the hairs on his neck stand on end.

Tina clutched Phil's arm and stared in the direction Jim Bridger was looking. "We can't just stand here in the open," whispered Tina through dry lips.

"You're right, little girl." Codge gave Jim Bridger a command and they disappeared behind the shed.

Blaze nickered, nodding his head up and down. Tina could tell Blaze knew other horses were nearby.

"We'll hide behind the barn," said Phil urgently as he grabbed Ginger's reins.

Tina ran beside him, Blaze at her heels. A cat streaked across in front of her and Tina bit her lip to keep from screaming in alarm.

Waist-high weeds stood behind the barn. Mosquitoes buzzed angrily. A bumblebee flew from a crack in the barn.

"Tell me what's going on, Tina," whispered Phil close to her ear. "I want to know right now."

"I don't want to talk about it." Tears pricked her eyes, and she turned away so Phil couldn't see.

"You're going to talk about it, Tina. And you're going to talk right now. I want to know what's going on so I can try to stop it. Tell me, Tina!"

She wanted to ride away as fast and as far as she could, but she stood beside him and told him what Dallas had planned.

Phil frowned. "Sometimes Carl carries a gun. If they know we're here, they won't be able to let us go."

Tina stared up at him, her blue eyes wide with fear. "You mean they might kill us?" She gripped his arm. "And Codge?"

Phil nodded.

"We can't just stand here! I'm going to stop them." She wheeled around, weeds almost knocking her down, and sprung into the saddle. She kicked against Blaze and rode into the open. She heard Phil tell her to come back but she rode into the yard. Thunder cracked and lightning zigzagged across the sky.

"Go home, Tina!" shouted Dallas from Molly's back. Two boys rode beside him on spotted ponies. "Go now!"

Suddenly Phil was beside Tina. "We know your plans," shouted Phil. "We're going to go for the police."

Tina saw the anger on Larry's face as he kicked his pony into a run, heading right for them.

Codge stepped into the open, a shotgun to his shoulder. Jim Bridger stood at his side, growling menacingly. "You boys turn around and go back where you came from."

Larry pulled his pony up short as Dallas and Carl did the same. Tina saw the fear on Dallas's face. She wanted to shout at him she had told him so, that it would not work.

Codge held his shotgun ready, his face dark with rage. "You young whippersnappers think all you need to do to strike it rich is rob an old coot like me. You can't have my money. Go home before I pull this trigger like my finger's itching to do!"

Tina saw Carl's hand move and she knew he was going for a gun. She kicked Blaze and yelled for Codge to watch out. Blaze reared, frightening Carl's pony and sending Carl to the ground in a heap, his gun sailing into a clump of weeds.

Tina nudged Blaze back beside Ginger. She saw the anger on Phil's face as he glared at her. She turned her head away, her heart hammering.

THIRTEEN

The
Chase

Tina licked her dry lips as she watched Carl get awkwardly to his feet. Dust covered him from his curly brown hair down to his scuffed shoes.

"You boys are lucky Tina and Phil are here," said Codge gruffly as he continued pointing his shotgun at Dallas, Carl, and Larry. "I'd as soon shoot you as spit on you." Codge shifted his chew of tobacco into his other cheek. "You got two minutes to get out of my sight. I'm going to report this to the police this time. Next time, if there is a next time, I'll shoot your heads off."

Tina shivered, knowing Codge meant what he said. She looked at Dallas as he slumped in the saddle. Why hadn't he listened to her? She wanted to say something to him but she couldn't find any words.

Jim Bridger barked as the boys rode down the lane, leaving only a cloud of dust. Codge commanded the dog to be quiet and he crouched down next to Codge's feet.

The sky darkened and lightning flashed. Tina gripped the saddle horn as the thunder boomed. Blaze trembled and she patted him reassuringly.

"Do you think they'll be back, Codge?" asked Phil as he leaned forward on Ginger's back.

Codge shook his head. "They won't. Me and Jim Bridger'll go into the house out of the storm and we won't worry about a thing. Me and Jim Bridger have been taking care of ourselves a lot of years. We'll be just fine. You kids go home."

"When will you call the police?" asked Tina.

Codge picked up Carl's gun and emptied the chamber. "I won't bother the police. I just wanted to scare those boys. I don't want them knowing I didn't call the police. Let 'em sweat it out."

For Dallas's sake Tina was glad this wouldn't be on his record. Maybe he'd get smart and not try such a dumb thing again.

"Let's go, Tina. It looks like we might get caught in a downpour." Phil looked up at the sky with a frown. "Maybe it'll hold off until we get home."

"See you later, Codge." Tina turned Blaze and rode down the lane. She peeked at Phil beside her. Was he still angry at her?

"I know what you're thinking, Tina. If I

could've, I'd have skinned you alive when you rode against Carl. You could have been hurt!" He pushed his free hand through his blond curls. "You do crazy things, Tina, and I want to shake you."

"I couldn't let Carl pull his gun on Codge." Tina turned in her saddle to Phil. "Don't you see, Phil? None of this would have happened if I'd just found a way to stop Dallas. When will I ever do anything right?"

Phil's eyes narrowed. "Are you going to drop Dallas now?"

Tina's face turned a dull red and she squirmed uncomfortably. "Mind your own business."

"You can't still like the guy after today!"

Tina lifted her rounded chin. Why couldn't she admit that she did not want to see Dallas Tromley again?

"You are the most stubborn girl I've ever met!" Phil's hazel eyes snapped angrily. "You can't admit when you're wrong. Grow up, Tina!"

"Look who's talking? You're only two years older than I am. Are you all that grown up, Phil Rhyner? You might try to act like a man, but you're still a kid."

"At least I know my age. I don't have to put on a big act like you try to do."

She had never seen him so angry. She trembled. She wanted him to talk quietly to her and help her relax after the terrible experience with Dallas, Carl, and Larry.

At the end of the lane they rode at a gallop across the Lambert land toward the ranch house. The wind shifted directions and blew coldly against Tina. She leaned close against Blaze.

Suddenly Phil reached out and grabbed Blaze's bridle. Tina jerked up in alarm, her eyes wide.

"Look!" Phil pointed toward a clump of cottonwoods. Tina could barely make out three horses hidden.

"What is it?" she asked, her heart racing. She could tell by Phil's face that he was frightened.

"It's Dallas and his friends, and I don't think they want to pass the time of day with us. We'll have to ride the other way."

"Maybe they want to talk."

"They want *us*, Tina." A muscle jumped in his jaw. "Ride, Tina, like you've never ridden before. We can't let them catch us."

Terror gripped her as she imagined what the boys could do to them. She whipped Blaze into a run just as Phil yelled that Dallas had seen them and was after them.

Tina looked back and her heart zoomed to her feet as she recognized Molly and the spotted ponies. Wind whipped her hair into her face. Ginger's pounding hooves blended with Blaze's. How close were the others? Could Molly and the spotted ponies run faster than

Blaze and Ginger, who were tired from running earlier?

Giant drops of cold rain hit Tina's arms and face, then poured from the sky, soaking her. Her shirt clung to her. She knew they could not make it home. The mine on Tanner Hill seemed the only means of escape from the rain and Dallas and his friends.

Phil had the same idea as he raced ahead of her in the direction of Tanner Hill. Tina followed. Maybe Dallas would give up and turn back.

At Tanner Hill she dropped from Blaze's back. She knew Blaze would continue to run with the reins hooked over the saddle horn. She'd trained him that way for trick riding. Frantically she scrambled up the hill to the mine entrance with Phil beside her. If only Dallas, Carl, and Larry would follow Blaze and Ginger a ways before they would see the saddles were empty.

Tina stood thankfully inside the mine out of the cold rain. "Are we safe?" she asked hoarsely as she reached for Phil.

He caught her hand and held it firmly. "Only for a while. We're going to find the back entrance to this mine."

She shivered. "*If* there is one!"

"Yes. But we can't stay here, because we'll have company soon enough. Our little trick will keep them away only for a while." She could hear he was tense and frightened. "Let's go, Tina. Don't let go of me. It's important that we stay together."

"I wish we had a light. I don't think I can walk back in the mine without a light." Fear pricked her skin and a sick knot tightened in her stomach.

"You can do it because you have to." He pulled her and she was forced to walk with him. She stumbled when he started to run.

"Don't run!" she cried, pulling back, but he jerked her arm and said they had to.

"We know the area we've explored doesn't have holes or turn-offs. I can judge when to stop and walk slowly."

She had to trust his judgment. She wanted to jerk free and run out of the mine and take her chances with Dallas. He wouldn't really do anything to hurt her, would he? She could not answer that.

Suddenly Phil tripped and Tina fell on top of him. Her chin struck his head and she cried out in pain.

"It's that store dummy," said Phil impatiently.

"Tina!"

Tina jerked up, her heart racing. Dallas was calling her. She felt for Phil's hand and gripped it tightly.

"Tina! If you can hear me, come out now! I'm here alone. Carl and Larry left. Come out and let's talk."

"Don't trust him," whispered Phil.

"I won't!" She waited for what seemed hours. Had they given up and gone home? Were they this minute walking into the mine searching for them? A light bobbed and she gripped Phil tighter.

"Let's go," he said against her ear. "I'm going to use this dummy to feel our way."

She walked along with him, her heart in her mouth. What if there was no back door? They would catch her and Phil and kill them here in the mine. No one would ever find them. Tears stung her eyes. This was a terrible way for her life to end! Would Dad try to find her, or would he be so busy with Mary that he wouldn't care?

Phil stopped and she bumped into him. "They're closer, Tina," he said close to her ear. His breath tickled her and she shivered. "We'll have to run."

Tina pushed her wet hair out of her face as Phil pulled her into a run. What if they ran into a hole? She forced the thought away. They must run fast! They could not be caught by Dallas, Carl, and Larry!

FOURTEEN

Help

Tina stumbled and would have fallen but for Phil's firm grip on her hand. A sharp pain shot through her side and she bit her lip to keep from crying aloud.

Phil stopped so abruptly that Tina knocked into him. Nervously she looked behind her. She could not see a bobbing light. Had the boys left? Or had they turned off the light so they could sneak up on them? She shivered, pressing against Phil for comfort.

"Tina," he whispered. "We can't do this alone. We can't get away without help."

"Who will help us?" She felt a wild fear rising inside her and she knew in a minute she'd be screaming and screaming with no way to stop herself.

"God is always with us. He's our strength and our help."

Tina held her breath. Phil sounded so sure of himself.

"Father," Phil prayed softly with his head pressed against Tina's. "I thank you for your protection. Stop Dallas and those boys from finding us. Make them turn around and leave this mine. Thank you for the angels that guard us. Take away our fear and make us brave because you are in control of our lives."

An overwhelming peace settled over Tina. She waited for the fear to return but it was gone! Nothing like this had ever happened to her before.

"Lead us out of this mine safely and help us reach home safely. Thank you, Father. I love you. Tina does too."

Tina bit her bottom lip as tears pricked her eyes. Did she love God? Did he love her?

Phil moved his head away and Tina wanted to press against him again to keep the protected feeling that enveloped her. To her surprise she still felt protected. She had never really believed that God knew who she was or where she was. But he'd answered Phil's prayer. God must know. He must care. Tina felt the way she did when she was close to her dad. She *knew* nothing could harm her now.

"Let's go, Tina." Phil's voice was sure and strong. "We have nothing to fear. We're going to get out of this mine and get home."

She walked with him for a while in silence. For the first time she could understand why Dad had been so glad to learn of God. "Phil."

She waited and he slowed to almost a snail's pace. "Phil, I do love God. And I know he loves me! I want to know Jesus as my Savior like you and Dad do."

"Wait, Tina." He stopped and she felt his hand tighten around hers. "Don't say that just because you're scared."

She smiled, then realized he couldn't see her face. "Phil, you've been after me for months now. I guess I didn't believe what you told me. Now I do."

"Are you teasing me, Tina? This is too important to tease about."

"I'm serious, Phil. I wouldn't tease about this. All I know is that I was scared to death, and now I'm not because I know God is with us, helping us. I know we'll get home safe." She couldn't believe she was saying this. She thought back and realized she'd wanted to become a believer the night Rita had. Tina smiled. Rita would be very surprised.

Phil stopped. "I don't see anyone following us. Maybe we should go back that way."

"Maybe we should." She waited to know what Phil was going to do.

Finally he said, "We'll continue the way we're going, Tina."

Dust drifted up from Phil pushing the dummy ahead of him in the darkness. Tina sneezed, her head jerking forward. She pulled her wet shirt away from her skin and wished it would dry even a little.

"You weren't making fun of me because I prayed, were you, Tina?"

She squeezed his hand and felt an answering squeeze. "I wasn't, Phil. I heard you say a lot of times that a person could pray anytime, anywhere. I've prayed inside myself about becoming a Christian. I did it just the way you said to pray before. I don't know what I can say to convince you that I mean it."

"It's just so sudden!"

"It just *seems* sudden, Phil. I've been fighting against giving in for a long time. I can't understand why I did unless it was because I was sort of mad at God. It seemed like he was coming between my dad and me—just like Mary was. But now I know God loves me! And I love him. Since my mom died I've had a hard time loving anyone."

"And you just had to pick on Dallas Tromley when you finally did learn to love."

Tina sighed. "I'm sorry, Phil." She paused. "Phil, why did it hurt you for me to like Dallas?" Her heart raced as she waited for his answer.

"Tina! Look—just ahead! A tiny light!"

Tina released Phil's hand and started ahead of him but he grabbed her by the shirttail, then the arm.

"Don't run! We have to feel our way ahead."

"Oh, Phil! We're going to get out of here! I can't wait to breathe fresh air again. I wonder if the rain stopped. I wonder if Dallas went home." She smiled at the freedom from fear.

"What will you do when you see him again?"

"I don't know. I do know I'll never go with him again."

"I'm glad!"

"Are you going to write to Rita, Phil?"

"Maybe."

She licked her dry lips and walked several steps in silence. "Do you like Rita?"

"Yes."

"Oh." Tina didn't want him to like Rita. She wanted him to like her. She stopped and Phil jerked her arm.

"What's wrong?"

"Nothing! Nothing at all!" Why hadn't she realized that she liked Phil better than she'd ever liked Dallas Tromley? She liked working, riding, hiking, fishing, and just talking with Phil. She liked the way he smiled and the way he flexed his muscles to show her each new development.

"Oh, Tina! We made it!"

Tina blinked in surprise as Phil pushed aside the tree branch that drooped across the opening.

She stood outside with Phil and breathed in the fresh air. The rain had stopped but a cool breeze blew against her, making her shiver. She laughed in delight. Who cared about the cold? They were out in the open! They were free!

Phil rested his hands on her shoulders and looked into her face. "I want to see for myself that you meant it when you said you accepted Jesus."

She smiled into his hazel eyes. Oh, he had nice eyes! "I mean every word, Phil. I'm sorry for all the bad things I've said and done to you while you were praying for me. Forgive me."

"I do, Tina." He smiled and she wanted to hug him. "Steve and Mary will be very happy." He frowned. "I hope they aren't worried about us."

"How long will it take us to get home?" She looked around, trying to get her bearings. Her eyes widened. "Look, Phil! We're almost in Codge's backyard!"

Phil laughed. "My heavenly Father does a great job taking care of us." He caught Tina's hand and they ran together across the prairie grass.

Jim Bridger barked loudly until Codge walked out of his house. He pushed his hat to the back of his head. "Me and Jim Bridger were just considering going to look for you. Steve drove in a while ago and said your horses came home empty. You kids jump in my truck and I'll have you home sooner than you can shake a stick."

Tina wanted to hug Codge but she knew he would be embarrassed. She climbed in the truck and smiled as Phil slid in beside her.

"Your face is dirty, Tina."

She laughed. "So is yours."

"But you're still pretty."

She sat back with a smile as Codge drove the noisy truck down his lane.

■ FIFTEEN ■

A Bright
New Day

Tina jumped out of bed, smiling happily. Dad had hugged her very close last night when she'd climbed out of Codge's truck. Mary had stood back and Tina had wanted to tell her that she didn't hate her, but the words wouldn't come. Mary had sent her into a hot shower, then tucked her into a warm bed. Steve had grimly said he'd take care of Dallas, Carl, and Larry.

By the time Tina was dressed in jeans and a green plaid shirt she was starved. Had Phil slept as soundly as she had? Had his uncle taken as good care of him as Mary and Dad had of her?

Tina leaned close to the mirror as she brushed her long brown hair. It was nice having a mother fuss over her. She wrinkled her nose playfully. Was it really Tina Lambert thinking that?

She turned at a soft knock on the door.
"Come in."

"Why are you out of bed?" asked Mary sharply, but with a smile. "I was all ready to play the big mother role and you didn't give me a chance."

Tina laughed and Mary joined in. "Mary, will you forgive me for being so mean to you? I want to try to be a good daughter to you."

Mary's eyes filled with tears. "I want to be a good mother to you, Tina. I promise not to come between you and your father."

Tina could see she meant it. "I don't want to come between you and Dad either, Mary. I'll ask Jesus to teach me to act the way I should. I've forgotten how to be in a real family with a mom, dad, and daughter."

"We'll learn together." Mary stepped forward, her hands out, a question in her brown eyes.

Tina smiled and walked into her arms. It felt wonderful to be hugged and loved by Mary. She looked up to find Dad standing in the open doorway, a wide smile on his face.

"I'm happy to see my two best girls together this morning." He walked to them and took one in each arm, smiling from one to the other. Tina didn't mind sharing him at all. She smiled. She was already learning about love.

"Phil's been asking about you for almost two hours," said Steve, grinning. "I told him that Mary wouldn't let me wake you up for chores."

"Where is he now?" asked Tina breathlessly.

"I sent him fishing. I told him you'd probably be in bed until noon. I didn't think after yesterday, you'd want to get up so early." Steve kissed her cheek. "I'm so glad you're home. I couldn't be happy without you. Those boys, Carl and Larry left town. And Mrs. Tromley said she'd see to Dallas!"

Tina stood on tiptoe and kissed his cheek. He smelled like the after-shave lotion she'd bought him last Christmas. She didn't want to think about Dallas. "Would you care if I went fishing with Phil?"

"I'd like you with me a while, honey." Steve pulled her to his side. "Can't that boy wait?"

"Daddy, I need to talk to him."

"All right. I can spare you for a while." He kissed her again, then let her go. "I'd like to keep you a little girl forever, but I know I can't. Have fun fishing."

"I will." Tears sparkled in her eyes as she walked to the door.

"How about taking a picnic lunch?" asked Mary.

Tina turned with a wide smile. "I'd like that!"

"You saddle Blaze and I'll pack a lunch."

Tina rushed across the room and hugged Mary tightly. "Thanks, Mary. I'll be back in a flash!"

Several minutes later Tina rode toward the stream where she'd always fished with Phil. A warm breeze blew against her and she held her face up to it. What a perfect day! What a beautiful day!

She touched the knapsack strapped to her side. She'd put in something special for Phil.

Ginger stood with her nose down in the grass. Phil sat under a large cottonwood, his back pressed against the trunk. He didn't have his fishing pole out of its case.

"Hi, Phil," she called gaily as she jumped off Blaze. She saw his surprise and laughed.

"I thought you were going to sleep forever!" He walked toward her, his eyes sparkling. "Did you get enough rest? Are you really all right?"

"I'm rested. I'm fine. I'm happy, Phil!" She shrugged off the knapsack and rested it against the tree. "Why aren't you fishing?"

He stuffed his hands into his jeans. "I didn't feel like it. It's not much fun going alone."

"I know. But you aren't alone now." She walked to the edge of the clear stream. "Did you watch for any frogs?"

"I saw a couple of big ones."

She turned to him and touched his shirt pocket. "But you didn't catch one to carry around, I see."

He laughed. "Not this time. Don't you think I'm too old for that?"

She shook her head. "Nope. And neither am I. It's fun catching frogs. I've found out I can be thirteen and still have fun like I did when I was twelve." She took a deep breath and locked her fingers together. "I was trying to be someone else when I was with Dallas. It's different with you. You like me just the way I am. Don't you?"

He rested his hands on his hips and studied her with his head tipped. "Most of the time I do." After a moment, he laughed. "I'm teasing. I think you're great!"

She flushed with pleasure. "Are you going to write to Rita?" She had really wanted to ask if he liked her better than Rita.

"Sure. She asked me to.'

Tina watched a fish jump. "She likes you a lot."

"I like her a lot. And Rob too." He tugged her hair. "What are you trying to say, Tina? You and I are friends. Don't be afraid to say what you really mean."

She looked up at him, her hands at her sides. "Phil, I like you a lot. I like you better than anyone else." She stopped and couldn't go on. What if she asked him if he liked her best and he said no? Phil wouldn't lie even to make her feel better.

He caught her hand and held it. "Tina, I like you best, too. I have for a long time."

"You do? You have?"

He smiled and she felt weak all over. "I love you, Tina."

"You do?" Her eyes sparkled and she wanted to hug him.

Suddenly he dropped her hand. "I'm hungry. What did you bring to eat?" He walked to the knapsack and Tina followed with a frown.

Why had he suddenly dropped her hand and changed the subject? She had wanted to tell him that she loved him. Maybe he'd been afraid she was going to and he hadn't wanted to hear it.

Tina opened the knapsack and handed Phil a chicken sandwich and slices of cucumber from the garden. "I brought you something special," she said.

"What?"

"It's not as good as dill pickles, but you'll think so." She pulled out a plastic bag and handed it to him. She watched his face as he opened the bag and pulled out a handful of chocolate covered malted milk balls. Did he feel like she had when he'd brought a jar of dill pickles for her?

He dropped the malted milk balls back in the bag and set the bag down.

"Don't you like them?" Tina felt close to tears. She'd wanted to bring something that he especially liked.

He took her hand. "Tina, I think your gift is great. Thank you." He smiled at her and then looked away quickly. Tina noticed that his face was flushed under his tangled blond hair.

She could tell he had something more to say and was having a hard time saying it. "What is it, Phil? You're always telling me to say what I really mean. You can say what you want to. I'll try not to be hurt."

"Tina, I want to kiss you." She felt her cheeks grow red. "I've never kissed a girl and it scares me."

"Don't be afraid of me. I'm Tina. Remember?" She felt fluttery inside as he leaned toward her. She closed her eyes and kissed him back as he kissed her. "I love you, Phil."

He smiled. "Will you go with me when Steve says you're old enough?"

She nodded. "I think he's beginning to think I'm growing up."

"I think you are too." He grinned. "Just don't grow up too fast or you'll pass me up."

"I wouldn't do that."

He opened the bag of candy and pulled out a chocolate ball.

Tina laughed happily as he cracked it apart with his sharp teeth. A large bull frog hopped in the grass nearby. "Oh, Phil! Look! Quick, catch him." She scrambled after Phil as the frog leaped again.